EVE

EVE

A Novel

Evelyn Minshull

CARMEL • NEW YORK 10512

This Guideposts edition is published by special arrangement with HarperSanFrancisco Publishers.

INTERIOR DESIGN BY RICHARD KHARIBIAN

Library of Congress Cataloging-in-Publication Data

Minshull, Evelyn.
    Eve : a novel / Evelyn Minshull.—1st ed.
      p.   cm.
    ISBN 0-06-065766-9
    1. Eve (Biblical figure)—Fiction. I. Title.
PS3563.I476E94   1990
813'.54—dc20   89-45935
                              CIP

---

90 91 92 93 94 HAD 10 9 8 7 6 5 4 3 2 1

To the memory of Lois T. Henderson
for the inspiration of her friendship

Part I

One

In the beginning, there were colors, swirling and brightening, and a bubbling, buzzing, humming—unlike anything she had known before.

She was sure of that.

She retraced memory, but lazily. Except for an insistent rhythm that still throbbed gently at temple, wrist, and throat, she met only soft, black silence.

Nothingness.

But it didn't matter. Soft pressure nudged toward intensified color and sound, and she knew exhilaration. Expectancy. Excitement. The past, or lack of it, became unimportant. She yearned toward the evolving present . . . and opened her eyes.

Later, she would think how fitting it was that she had seen Him first, then the man who would be known to her as Adam. God loomed above her, large but not frightening, with a shine about Him. He was smiling, and she returned the smile.

"It is good," He said.

She nodded—not understanding, but knowing that she would have nodded whatever He had said. Or if He had said nothing at all.

The man lay on his side, snoring lightly. His hair was bright and slightly curling. She looked at her arm for comparison and saw that his skin was a bit darker than hers. A faint tinge of pink arched the bridge of his nose. Sunlight struck sparks of gold from his body hair, so fine she wouldn't have noticed them except for that burnishing.

Warmth stirred within her at the sight of him. For the larger presence, God, she felt something quite different, perhaps a greater respect in response to His aura of power. For the man—no longer snoring, but rousing from sleep, rubbing his eyes as she had rubbed her own—she felt kinship, as though she had known him before. Almost as though they were in some way joined.

"You are," God said, speaking to her unspoken thought. Then He reached His hand to the waking man and helped him to his feet.

With a slow, graceful gesture, the man touched his side. His deep brown eyes, fringed with golden lashes, widened then narrowed and widened once more, as though shaping a silent question.

The throbbing enlarged within her, and she felt a tightening, a trembling; a reluctance, a yearning; a promise, a fear.

Smiling as though to reassure her, God answered the man's unframed question. "I have formed a companion for you."

The man turned. A faint flush touched his cheeks, and his eyes shone as he took her hands in his. His fingers, warm and firm, pressed hers almost to the point of pain.

Still, as she returned his clasp, joy surged within her. The insistent rhythm thundered in her ears.

"It was not good for man to be alone," God said.

Surprised by his voice they turned, and she thought, *The man forgot Him, just as I did.* A giggle bubbled in her throat.

"Do you remember, Adam," He continued, "how we considered the animals of the fields, of the streams, and the air, but found none fitting to be your close companion?"

"Yes. But this one—" and his clasp tightened further, "—*this* one is perfect!"

God nodded. "Both you and the animals were formed from the dust of the earth. Into you, alone, I breathed my own breath, to establish forever our kinship. But her . . . *her* I formed *from you.* From one of your own ribs."

Again, Adam's hand strayed to his side, though only briefly, before reclaiming hers once more. Solemnly, he whispered, "This is now bone of my bones, and flesh of my flesh. She shall be called Woman, because she was taken out of man."

Wo-man. Wo-man. She tasted the syllables in her mind. They were gentle and flowing, not altogether unpleasant. There was softness there, whereas *A-dam* communicated strength. And there was in her name—

She shook her head. She lacked experience to identify a mournfulness also suggested by the sounds.

And yet, what could that matter while the man Adam studied her with those glowing eyes, while she could feel a pleasurable current flowing from his fingertips to hers, thence through her whole body and back to him again?

It is good, she thought, unconsciously echoing God's earlier words.

"For this," Adam said gently, his lips soft and pliant, and his voice a caress, "For this a man shall leave all and cling only to his wife, and they shall be one flesh."

He felt it, too, then, this oneness she had sensed even as he woke. The rib. Before she was herself, she had been a part of him, close to his beating heart. Its rhythm was all she had known of any past. She was a part of him, and he of her, and both would be doubly complete because of their separateness.

"Come, let me show you all the things I've named!" Adam's voice was vibrant, eager. And his tugging at her hand was impossible to resist, even had she wanted to.

Adam proved an eager teacher. Words tumbling, sometimes a name temporarily forgotten, he hurried her from one wonder to the next. She must listen to the deepest tones of the frog, swelling his throat from the verge of the lily-studded pool. She must run her fingertips along the ridges of the crocodile's back. She must know the softness of gosling down against her cheek, share laughter at the ungainly strolling of a young giraffe, notice the tender green of the luna's wings, and sniff the fragrance of spired hyacinth.

She enjoyed running hand in hand with Adam along the moss-soft pathway, which wound among towering vines . . . resting on a sun-warm rock where lizards drowsed . . . dipping her toes in tepid pools, golden with flickering fish . . . wandering ankle-deep in meadow grasses, where lions grazed and stretched and yawned, and flamingos preened their ruby wings.

At last she and Adam sat, softly talking, while giant leaves threw sculptured shadows across their own.

"It's beautiful," she said. "Is it truly all yours?"

"Yes," he said. Then quickly, "No. It's mine—*ours*—to tend. To keep." He paused. "But it really belongs to *Him.*"

She sat quietly, watching a beetle scurry along a drooping palm frond.

Adam's hand on her forearm reclaimed her attention. "He told me that I—*we*—could eat from any of the trees of the Garden." He plucked a bulbous yellow fruit and proffered it. The aroma was ripe and mellow, and she inhaled deeply of it.

"Eat," he urged gently, touching the smooth skin to her lips.

Scarcely exhaling, she nibbled at it, then pressed her hands against his, forcing the fruit closer, sinking her teeth through the slight toughness into the juicy pulp. She made small sounds of pleasure, and his laughter was full and rich.

"Mmmmmmm," she murmured, taking another bite. Then she moved the dripping fruit toward Adam's lips. "You eat," she insisted softly.

Their glances held as he, too, sampled the juicy flesh. The tremor that swept her body was even more pleasurable than the taste had been. Absently, she drew her fingertips across her sticky chin.

"It is good," Adam said.

Instinctively, she knew that he spoke not alone of the fruit; that he sensed the same pleasures, the same confusions, as those which warmed her.

He looked away, and his hands fumbled awkwardly with the half-eaten fruit. "There are many, many others—" he faltered.

She had seen some of them. Full, purple orbs; round fruits with dimpled coverings; one long fruit, curved and golden; another freckled with spots of rust and brown; some clumped; others hard, encased in shells.

Sighing, she hugged her knees to her chin and rocked contentedly. "And we may eat from all of them?"

"From all but one."

For the first time, she felt a chill, deep inside. Before she could be certain that it had happened, it was gone. Her rocking resumed. "When there are so many," she said quietly, almost to herself, "what could one matter?"

If there was one spot in all the Garden that she loved more deeply than all others, it was the glade surrounding the smallest waterfall.

Adam preferred the power of the thunderous falls near the edge of the Garden. Sometimes she stood with him there, savoring the cool spray on her cheeks, but cringing a bit from the sound. There was so much of it! It assaulted her ears. She could feel its power thrumming along her nerves. The swift flow of water captured and fragmented the sunlight, creating prismatic designs, which danced and darted and delighted. But once she had tossed a leafy stem to it and winced as the wood was snapped, the leaves thrown high and torn.

In her mind, she compared Adam's waterfall to God, and her favorite, gentler one to Adam.

It wasn't that she'd ever heard God thunder and roar. She'd never seen Him destroy anything. Indeed, Adam often told how He had created all of the wonders of the Garden, and with what special tenderness He had formed Adam himself. And she remembered waking gently from her own creation.

It was only that she sensed in God a power, like that of the waterfall. He was her friend, and she loved Him. Both Adam and she walked easily with Him through the Garden—talking, sharing.

But while Adam was a part of Him, having drawn his very breath from God, she was instead a part of Adam.

She plucked a crimson flower, inhaled its fragrance, then tucked it behind her ear.

A part of Adam.

She smiled, touching her fingertips to fern fronds as she strolled along the pathway.

She knew such intensity when she and Adam were alone. There were times, as now, when she yearned for solitude that she might examine and appreciate her love for him in a manner impossible when he was touch-close, involving her senses and stirring her emotions.

Slender tendrils of shining water whispered from rock to rock.

Watching, she curled into her favorite mossy seat and inhaled the peace of the place. A bulky butterfly fanned past her cheek, wobbled close to the gliding water and clung, at last, to a swaying spire of sweet clover. Unseen birds purled their songs, and the purring and rhythmic grazing of nearby leopards added lulling patterns of their own.

Sinking more deeply into the moss, she rested her head against an inclining rock and closed her eyes. Already a longing for Adam had begun to stir at the base of her throat. She would return soon, perhaps walking through the center of the Garden where the Special Tree stood, and help him dress the vines. She enjoyed the texture of the branches, some young and firm, some frayed and woody, and the warm, smooth purpleness of grapes, hanging in heavy bunches. Some were out of reach, except to the chattering monkeys she never tired of watching.

Slashes of sunlight moved, reshaping lights and shadows. She breathed evenly, lips parted slightly, her hands relaxed in the moss.

She was wakened, gently, by the nudging head of a great white bear, asking to be petted.

Stretching, laughing, she mounted, delighting in the deep, soft pile of his pelt, and urged him toward the center of the Garden.

They paused, briefly, at some distance from the Special Tree. The Tree of the Knowledge of Good and Evil, God had called it. The one tree she and Adam were prohibited from using. If they ate of it, God had warned, they would "surely die"—whatever that meant. God had shaped the words a bit grimly, and she'd hugged herself against the chill the warning brought.

The bear danced uneasily, muttering, apparently eager to be off. But she sat, head tilted, and observed the tree. She thought it not special at all. The fruit seemed ordinary, not nearly as inviting as pomegranates or succulent golden pears. The foliage lacked the delicacy of locust, the ornateness of fig, the slender beauty of palm, the variety of sassafras.

At the pressure of the bear's great head against her knee, and the prodding of her need for Adam's company, she turned from the tree, her thoughts racing ahead to the Place of Vines.

The days evolved lazily, in a slow, warm manner, the pace altering only as she and Adam chose to alter it. Sometimes, after hours of tugging spent leaves from various vines, of encouraging strong young shoots to root themselves in loosened soil, they would drop their work and race to the stream, to frolic there; or climb palm trees, mimicking the chatter of monkeys; or gather from the Garden floor bright scraps of color—lost plumage, fallen hibiscus petals, vivid pebbles.

Later they might rest in some quiet glade where running water murmured, and birdsongs carved bright, crystalline slashes through the silence. Adam might weave for her a crown of strong meadow grasses and stud it with jewel-like chicory, anemone, or edelweiss. And she might tickle his sunburned nose with timothy, or tenderly feed him watercress or blueberries.

In the evenings, when God walked with them, they might commune in quietness, their companionship enough. Though sometimes, as God sat with them beside the stream where trout competed languidly for some falling seed or berry, He would tell them once again the story they never wearied of hearing: how each step of Creation had occurred, how He had delighted in diversity and detail, and how He had crowned achievement with His most loving designs—Man, then Woman.

"You are made in our image," He assured them. "You breathe with our breath, and we have blessed you, giving you dominion over all this creation . . . over the fish of the sea, and the fowl of the air, and over every living thing which moves upon the earth."

So many creatures, she would exult, counting the species just within her view. *So much power.*

But God still spoke. "You will multiply, filling the earth. You will be fruitful, as this earth is fruitful—furnishing herbs bearing seed for food, and trees bearing fruit which yield seed. For you, and for all these creatures you command, there is food." He paused, then added in a soft breath of satisfaction, "It is very good."

Yes, she thought, content. *It is all good.* And leaning against Adam's strong, warm arm she shared a smile with God. He had given them so much, asking only that they keep His beautiful Garden, and use it freely.

Except for that one tree, which He seldom mentioned, having told them so firmly that it was denied them.

Sometimes she wondered why, when He had showered them with so many gifts, He had withheld one tree. Could it be that the rather ordinary-looking fruit tasted so exceptional that He wanted it only for Himself?

She tried to imagine a fruit juicier than the golden-ripe pear, more dramatic than the pomegranate, sweeter than melon.

Or might the fruit of that Special Tree be unfit for their eating—sour, perhaps, or dry and tasteless? But if that were so, why not just allow them to discover for themselves its inferiority?

She found it difficult, though, to imagine any of His creations as being less than marvelous and exciting.

Just then she caught His glance, and read concern in His tones as He repeated the warning. "Of every tree of the Garden, you may freely eat. But of the Tree of the Knowledge of Good and Evil, you shall not eat of it. For the day that you eat of it, *you shall surely die.*"

She shivered, hugging herself.

There was so much that He said that she couldn't understand. Usually, it didn't trouble her. Usually, she listened to the rhythms of His voice and felt comfort there, and it was enough.

But what did it mean to die? And what was *evil*? And *why* was that one tree different? So important? So . . . intriguing?

The serpent's eyes were like round black pebbles, polished under water. There was all about him a glow.

He gazed at her from the Special Tree. She had never seen him there before. She had, in fact, never seen him anywhere. There had been other serpents sleeping among the vines, their patterned coils blending with the mottled greens, or moving placidly from food to sunning-spot.

But there was nothing placid about this serpent. His eyes were alive and active. His crimson tongue flicked with what seemed to be excitement.

Something within her said to move on quickly.

But something stronger held her there.

If Adam were only here . . . But did she want Adam to stand between her and the serpent for protection, or to stand beside her, sharing this unusual event?

"It was you," the serpent said softly, "*you* I wanted to meet."

Her cheeks flushed with pleasure, and she decided that she didn't need Adam at all.

"I have been curious," he continued, adjusting his coils.

Almost hypnotically, she watched the shifting patterns. How beautiful he was! How poised! Unconsciously, she imitated the grace of his movements as she relaxed, sinking to a large flat rock.

"Your position here is quite enviable," he murmured, and she nodded, not even wondering what envy might be. "God has given all of this Garden to you, is that not correct?"

"Yes," she answered.

"You are to have dominion over all living creatures. Is that not true?"

"Yesss." Unconsciously, she had adopted his sibilance.

"That would mean, would it not, that you could command me, as well?"

She frowned slightly. "I . . . suppose so." *Yes, surely,* she thought, since he moved along the branch of the tree, and so could move over the earth, he would be under her power. Hers and *Adam's,* she amended swiftly, a bit uncomfortably. She shifted on the rock.

His voice lulled her as he recited, "You have dominion over the fish of the sea . . . and over the fowl of the air . . . and over everything that creeps upon the earth . . ."

"Yes . . . yes . . . yessss . . ."

He smiled, and slowly she returned the smile.

"God must love you very, very much."

She nodded, her heart warming with that knowledge.

"Because of this great love, He would be unable to deny you anything you truly desired."

Again, she nodded, then stiffened a bit as she remembered the tree—the very tree in which the serpent rested, undulating slightly.

That small chill she had known before flickered deep within. She should leave, she knew. Adam might be looking for her—

"You have drunk the cool milk of the coconut, and tasted its white flesh."

She relaxed.

"You have exulted in the sweetness of papaya."

She smiled, remembering.

"Have you eaten yet . . . of the fruit of *this* tree?"

She shook her head unevenly.

"Not yet?" His voice had softened with surprise. "Perhaps it had not yet occurred to you? Perhaps it has seemed unpleasant to you? Perhaps *now* you might try it, taking some to the Man for his enjoyment!"

She cleared her throat. "It is true," she said, "that we may eat of the trees of the Garden. But of the tree which is in the midst of the Garden God has said, 'You shall not eat of it, *neither shall you touch it,* lest you die.' " Abruptly, she stood, edging backward from the rock. She should never have ventured so close.

He was laughing! Soundlessly, shaking with mirth, the serpent was laughing! At *her!*

She insisted a bit stiffly, "Well, that *is* what He said."

"Yes . . . Yesss . . . I have no doubt." He seemed to be making a genuine effort toward control. "It's only that"—he paused, straightening, and then seemed to shake himself free of the laughter—"it's only, my dear Woman," he said, "that you wouldn't *really* die."

"But God said—"

"Oh, I never doubt that He *said* it. But that isn't what would happen at all. The fruit is quite delicious."

She frowned. Had she been correct, then, in supposing that God was saving it for Himself alone?

"However," the serpent continued matter-of-factly, "there is more involved than taste. God simply fears that when you eat of this fruit, your eyes will be opened, and you will be like Him."

God, afraid? Ridiculous! "We are already made in His image," she replied uncertainly.

How had she thought the tree ordinary before? How had she imagined its leaves less beautiful than those of other trees? In truth, its fruit glowed temptingly among glistening foliage, and she could, she thought, catch inviting suggestions of a marvelous aroma—ripe, pulsing . . .

The serpent yawned. "In his image? Yesss. Poor imitations, of course, lacking His power. His knowledge." He paused. "Haven't you sometimes wondered just what 'evil' is?"

She squirmed.

He was smiling again, his tongue flicking so swiftly that the forked end blurred.

"Is not the tree pleasant to look upon? Inhale that fragrance! Mmmmmmmmmmmm. Do you not yearn for wisdom? Ahhhhh! This fruit here is ripe, I believe."

Slowly, she stepped closer, and a branch brushed her shoulder. She drew back, but the glow, the beauty of the fruit drew her closer. And, under it all, the serpent's soft syllables wound enticingly. "Note the blush on the cheek. The flesh is meatier than anything else in the Garden, I believe. See how the cheek curves from the stem? Can you actually believe that God would deny this delight? He who shares so abundantly, who has shown His love for you through every word and action? Ah! The aroma! If you plan not to eat it, then certainly I shall, for the aroma, the color, the texture are too much for me. But you will, I believe, take it? Yesss. Yesss. I thought so. Here, touch it to your lips, your teeth, and savor the moment . . ."

Adam rested by the stream, his toes rippling the water.

She called his name softly, exultantly, and he turned, his gladness pure and naked in his eyes, in his gentle smile.

"Look!" She held out the fruit. "The serpent sent it to you!"

A frown twisted his brows. "But isn't that—?"

"Yess!"

His frown deepened.

"But it's *good!*" she insisted. "Truly, it is! I tasted it, and *I* haven't died. The serpent said that God couldn't really care and—*Oh! Adam!* It's better than any of the others!"

"But God said—"

"Oh, I *know* what He said!" Her voice sharpened with impatience. But it wasn't *true!* I'm not sure *why* He lied to us. Why don't you ask Him this evening? But the fruit is fine. Excellent, in fact!" Her expression softened. "Here . . . taste. See for yourself."

Nothing could ever again be the same.

Knowledge began even as Adam finished the fruit with gluttonous enthusiasm, met her glance, and then—grimacing—spat the sucked-clean seed to the earth. The uneasy animals kept a wide perimeter. Was it only in her imagination that the grass seemed wilted there, the pebbles lusterless, the earth somehow barren?

A swift shame engulfed her. Awkwardly, she sought to cover herself from the new and disturbing knowledge in Adam's eyes: shock, anger, lust, confusion, and fear.

Then, miserably, he said, "We are naked."

It was a shame they shared.

Having tasted alienation, however momentary, she was grateful even for this bleak moment of sharing. Separate and stumbling, they followed a pathway where once they had run easily, hand in hand. Now, tendrils snagged her hair. The vines seemed closer, hostile; the ground less even. Heat pressed against and within her. Her breathing labored. A bumblebee, dawdling across her path, sent her veering, stubbing her toe on a rock, scratching the flesh of her arm on rough bark, releasing a thin line of bubbling red she had no time to interpret. Catching quick, painful gasps, she searched for the bee, then saw it angling toward a vivid bloom. Leaning against the bole of a sycamore for support, she breathed more evenly. Adam's voice was touched with annoyance as he called back to her, and she answered, "The bee. I was afraid of the bee."

It sounded like foolishness in her own ears. Often, both she and Adam had encouraged the soft, bulbous creatures to their arms and shoulders. She had giggled as tickling feet traversed her flesh, and had exulted in firm furriness as she stroked a bee's small body.

Adam agreed wearily, "He might have stung you."

They knew that, now. Gathering herself to follow Adam once more, she wondered if the bees knew, too.

They hid near the greatest waterfall. The sound of the waters might cover their quickened breathing and the fear-heavy thudding of their hearts. God would surely never find them there—at least not in one evening's searching. Perhaps, by morning, the effects of the fruit would have dissipated—after all, they'd eaten little—and they could continue as before.

She hoped this could be possible. The weights of knowledge, of guilt, of sorrow and fear caught like half-swallowed plum pits in her throat.

Once, huddling there, touch-close to Adam but not touching, she wondered if the serpent had *known.*

And then she remembered his laughter.

Suddenly, she knew what evil was.

The serpent was evil.

Hatred boiled into her throat, bringing the taste of nausea. Then the sadness surged again as she recognized that *she* was evil, too. And she had thrust the evil upon Adam who, perhaps from his love for her, had also eaten of the damned fruit.

And yet, if he hadn't—

She moaned softly. If this guilt and fear had been hers alone to bear, while he continued in his innocence, could she have endured any of this? Better, indeed, to die, as God had threatened. She shivered slightly. But perhaps this *was* dying.

She shifted, uncomfortable in the fig-leaf coverings they had hurriedly fashioned, lest God come earlier than expected. The leaves were supple enough for shaping, and secure. But the ridged veins abused her tender breasts.

And her position was cramped.

She moved again. And sighed.

"Shh." Adam's hand gripped her forearm.

She strained her ears, hearing only the heavy music of the water. Peering from their hiding place, she saw the lions enter, stride, stretch. Muscles rippled beneath taut pelts. Never before had she guessed the strength in those muscles; never before had she interpreted that strength as potential danger. But the teeth were long and sharp. And the claws . . .

She shivered, closing her eyes. In her mind she could feel those claws ripping through flesh, and could hear her own imagined screaming. Her shaking increased, and Adam's hands, harsh on her shoulders, did nothing to assuage it. Perhaps she would never again be free of this fear, this trembling within her thoughts, this terror ingrained in her brain, these images of horror, superimposed across an Eden that seemed deceptively unchanged.

In the womb of Adam's rib cage, and later in the Garden, she had felt sheltered.

But now . . . now . . . now and forever—

Could safety truly be gone forever?

Could God be that angry, that cruel?

Eventually, because she was too exhausted for further trembling, she rested in Adam's rigid arms.

The waterfall thundered and drummed and roared.

Still, when God's footsteps and voice finally sounded in the Garden, she heard them—even above the violence of rushing water.

Two

Eve straightened from the dusty row, arching her back to calm dull thrusts of pain. Her fingertips, tender from thistle stings, prodded a muscle. In her womb, the child rumbled, rippling even the loose fur of her garment, already grown shoddy from wear, from grime, from night dews, from her sweat.

"You shall eat your bread in the sweat of your face," God had said in that terrible moment, long months before.

It seemed, each endless day, that everything they did was in the sweat of their faces, of their armpits and shoulder blades, of their aching thighs.

Wearily, she swiped at her chin and sought the shade of a young olive tree.

Again, the child moved. More comfortable, now, she could cover him with her hand and cherish God's promise, also delivered that bleakest of days, that ultimately her seed would triumph.

It troubled her, though, that only *she* had been mentioned, not Adam. And certainly this child had sprung from Adam's seed, as well. Could it be that God had spoken of another, later child?

No. She frowned with an intensity born of need. Surely, this was the child whom God had meant.

At the far end of a row, Adam worked silently. She heard the occasional scratch of stone on stony earth. The swish-rattle of the dried palm leaf he used to discourage gnats and flies. He worked steadily, but slowly. Joylessly.

How can it be otherwise? she thought bitterly. It was not only what they had lost that oppressed them, but what they failed to gain. Each day, they fought the same dogged battle with the stubborn earth, the relentless sun, the stones—which must surely multiply as they slept!—the ever-present thistles and thorns, the beetles that attacked the grain, and those marauding animals who moved in nighttime shadows, potential threat to Adam's small flocks. Each morning, the challenges and disappointments renewed. Each night, when coolness brought dew, though never enough to settle thoroughly the dust or encourage the young plants, her thoughts returned to Eden. To God.

Perhaps Adam's did, as well; they seldom spoke of Him. Perhaps Adam, too, cried deep within his rib cage: *Please! Please! Please! Please take us back!*

Or perhaps Adam asked only for his *own* return.

The thought brought pain, but she had learned to live with pain of many kinds. She watched him work, this man to whom she belonged as a grafted branch belongs to the mother tree. Nothing had decreased her love for him. If anything, that had grown stronger in this harsh new world they had inherited.

She'd dreamed the night before. Again. Much the same dream—or, rather, a waking from dreaming. She'd roused to her elbow, as she had done so many nights before, and the child had stirred, as though sharing her tension, her alertness. Surely, she'd heard God walking there, just beyond the silvering of moonlight. In the shadows. *There!* Hadn't the pattern altered, just a bit?

Her heart thumped, thudded, nearly stopped. Surely, *surely,* He was there! Almost, she touched Adam. But it would be too cruel to disappoint him further. She'd wait, until she was sure, until He stepped into full view.

While she'd strained her senses to catch that longed-for glimpse of Him, she'd planned what they might say to prove they'd learned obedience, at last.

Sighing, she left the olive shadow and returned to the staggered row of tender wheat.

Later—two rows later, a dozen scratches later, a thousand sighs later—she tugged at a young nettle, and snapped both it and the pale green wheat-stalk.

The nettle would renew from the root; the wheat and its promise were lost. Why were the thistles so hardy, the wheat so fragile? *Why?*

Sun-heat burrowed into her flesh, oppressing her. Why did the same sun encourage and nurture thornbushes, while the leaves of the olives and pears drooped? *Why?*

Glaring into the sun, daring it, she held that fractured wheat stem to her parched lips as though she had loved it, and rocked back and forth on her heels, her tears springing from deep, soundless sobs.

She sensed the scant shelter of shadow seconds before Adam's hands lifted her.

"My poor, dear Eve," he said, with a gentleness not always evident. "My poor, sweet girl."

He touched her forehead with his dry lips. Then her cheek, her neck, her lips.

"We've worked long enough, we three." One hand fell lightly to the bulge of the child. "It's time we rest. And eat." He led her past the field where date palms struggled; where olives, grayed by dust, shared space with brambles. They passed the stream where straggly ewes, as heavy with child as she, drank listlessly. Both she and Adam stepped a bit more briskly as they neared the shelter.

As always, she averted her glance, ducking quickly beneath the covering, into shadow.

Even after all these months, she mourned the animals slaughtered to provide that shade. She'd grown accustomed to the skins she and Adam wore. Indeed, those were so worn from constant rough usage that they scarcely resembled the lithe and vivid leopards they once had clothed. She had blocked from her mind the sight of their dying, the blood. The smell of it. The redness splashed like an obscenity across the vibrant green of Eden.

But when the awning moved in the wind, imitating life, when the spots of the giraffe rippled emptily and the zebra stripes billowed with that breeze and then collapsed, she always felt new sadness. And fresh guilt.

Adam helped her to the cot and, with soft murmurings, ordered her to rest.

When she awoke, there was milk, warm from the black goat who thought their tent was hers. There was cheese from the small skin kept cool in the stream. And there were thin wafers of bread, softened with honey.

She smiled, and Adam's eyes lit from deep within.

"It is good," she said, and took another small bite of the bread, now salty with the flavor of the sweat and tears that stained her lips.

During the night, a cooling wind moved in.

Eve woke, refreshed. She stretched, smiling, snuggling backward, closer to Adam's unconscious touch.

Though God was never visible, He seemed, on Seventh Days, at least closer. She could see His love of color in the waking sky, and in the welter of greens, drenched darker with dew. His music sang in the sounds of water and foliage, in the muted melodies of birds not quite awake.

As Adam was not quite awake.

She turned carefully, still smiling.

Adam.

How she loved him!

She tickled his nose with a strand of her hair, and both nose and mouth twitched.

Again.

And he jerked, snorting, but not waking.

When he had fully resettled, another tickle. He swiped crossly with a hand and grumbled.

And she giggled.

One eye opened. Then the other. "I knew I should have swatted harder," he teased and did. Smartly, to her rump.

"*Ahhhh!*" With an agility she'd thought lost, perhaps forever, she flipped to her knees and her hand found a sandal. While Adam protected his face, making mock cries of terror, she thumped him repeatedly. The child within her, seeming to enjoy this play, romped and prodded.

Tired but victorious, Eve knelt, gloating, the sandal bent double.

Adam pried it from her hand, examining it. "At least it's yours," he laughed. "If it splits and you bruise your foot, you suffer only what you deserve."

She nodded, smiling, needing nothing more than this closeness, which was more than physical.

Hands reaching behind his head, he loved her with his eyes.

For those moments, she had no thought of Eden. No regrets.

No anger. Not even guilt. Just the warm, glowing sensations of love felt, love given, love returned.

After the morning meal, they strolled beside the stream, counting the pregnant ewes.

Eve's favorite, Kara, came pattering to them, her belly swaying ponderously. Eve fondled the dainty head, stroked the stretching sides, answered eloquent bleats with her own soft words of reassurance.

As they continued into the meadow, Kara followed, her nose nuzzling Eve's knee, or reaching to her hand.

"You're worried, aren't you?" Adam asked, at last.

She nodded.

He plucked a desert rose, stripping its stem of thorns, and gave it to her. Absently, she tucked it in her hair.

"He'll be strong and healthy," he assured her. "And so will you."

She hadn't been concerned for herself; it had never occurred to her to be. It was for Kara she feared. Kara was too small, surely, for that growing bulk to escape. Eve knew momentary anger for the ram who had forced his seed within such a fragile frame. And for the God who had designed such a cruel system of reproduction.

As always, the blame turned inward. In Eden, animals had dropped their offspring effortlessly, painlessly. Marveling at the tiny features of cubs and foals and kittens, the down of chicks and cygnets, shaping gradually to feathers, Eve had wondered how their children would form, or if they would form at all, or simply appear one day—a small Adam, with sun-bright hair; a tiny duplicate of her, with dark hair long enough to sit on.

Or perhaps God must form each small girl from the rib of each Adam, as he had done with her.

The taste of forbidden fruit had dispelled forever such innocent fancies.

Now, she understood clearly the processes of initiation and fruition. And, she admitted to herself, it was not an altogether unsavory system.

Except that she worried for Kara . . .

Adam touched the petals of the rose in her hair, and she swung her attention to him.

"It will be good," he assured her. "I'll be with you. And God will be with us all."

Did he really believe that? she wondered. They passed from the meadow into a grove where palm leaves stirred and rattled, and sand shifted beneath their sandalled feet. Was he really still so very certain of God?

Perhaps, just as doubts stirred sometimes within her, they also wavered Adam's faith.

She shook herself, shedding deep thoughts. It was the Seventh Day, a day to rest the mind as well as the body.

Smiling at Adam, she suggested that they bathe in the stream. That they sit for a time, while their garments dried and sweetened, and watch fish dart for food. That they walk to the place where lilies bloomed and drink deeply of the fragrance. There, among the lilies, they might stand quietly close, sensing the rightness they had squandered in Eden, refreshing their souls for whatever the following days might bring of sweat and disillusionment, of pain and doubt.

The next week brought Kara's delivery.

They were in the field, fighting the brambles for berries that tasted meltingly like honey, when Eve heard her bleating.

"One of the lambs," guessed Adam, as he tied off a hide only half-full of berries, "caught somewhere."

But Eve knew at once that it was Kara.

He slung the bulging sack over his shoulder and set off on a trot.

Because of her awkwardness with the knot of her own sack, because of the weight of their child, because of the fear, which seized her heart and rendered her knees weak and nearly useless, she followed at a distance.

She heard in Kara's screams more than an ordinary panic and pain. An answering anguish rose into Eve's throat, but she choked it back, left the berries on a small rude table in their shelter, and found Adam and Kara in the shade of an almond tree. They worked together to free the lamb, its head already visible, but limp.

The ewe's head rolled, her glazed eyes seeming to find Eve. She bleated again, pleadingly, and tried to lurch to her feet. Adam's hands soothed her, but his worried glance found Eve's, and he shook his head.

They'd never lost a ewe before, not this way. To wild animals, yes, and that was bad enough. But to lose a mother in the violence of giving birth—

Dropping to her knees, Eve held and stroked Kara's damp head while Adam tugged and prodded at the opening, which strained and quivered and contracted.

"It will be over soon," Eve promised Kara gently, while Adam urged angrily, "Come out. Come! She has you ready. Give us some help!"

And the lamb did renew its struggle; did scramble and strain, bringing new frenzy to Kara's eyes and small, piteous mouth.

"I'm afraid—" Adam began, then sighed. "I know how much you love her. Perhaps—"

"If you were to reach inside—?"

"I might. But the pain—"

"If it saved her life, though." There was a catch in Eve's voice, though she'd tried to keep it even.

She watched for as long as she could bear to, then closed her eyes and dropped her face to Kara's, as though to absorb some of the gentle ewe's agony. She heard Adam's muttered urgings, his small sounds of straining, of frustration, of renewed determination. And, once, almost a sigh of surprise.

"It's coming, I think . . . yes! *Eve!* We have it! Another little ewe."

But Eve didn't turn to look. She couldn't have seen, anyway, through her tears. For she had known seconds before—when her fingertips sensed relaxation, when her cheek no longer felt that tiny, fanning breath—that Kara was dead.

She pushed ponderously to her feet. Her baby lurched within her, and she didn't reach to pat her belly. Could this child be plotting such evil for her? Could Adam's seed, delivered with loving violence, grow there, drawing from her the elements of its own strength and identity by sapping hers? Could it, like the lamb, attain its life at the expense of her own?

She numbed herself to Adam's demand for help. There was the cord to sever and tie. The afterbirth to clean. Lacking her mother, the lamb would require warmth and nourishment.

Eve had time for none of that, just then. First, the mourning, then the burial of Kara's fleecy shell in some spot safe from flies and vultures, *then* some help for Adam.

And for the lamb, if he insisted.

When she returned, Adam had already buried Kara, marking the spot with a spray of laurel. The lamb slept contentedly in a blanket of yellowed fleece, shorn months before.

Eve, willing that Adam continue its care, tried to ignore the lamb. But its vulnerability spoke to her. And when it stood uncertainly on stiff legs and called attention to its accomplishment with pride-filled bleats, Eve drew the lamb into her arms and nuzzled it. There was much of Kara there, rescued from death. A remnant of her, preserved.

From that day, they were inseparable. When Eve picked berries, Atra was there, selecting her own and complaining about the briars. When Eve weeded, the lamb helped—more drawn to the wheat, unfortunately, than to the nettles. When Eve ground grain, the lamb's nose was at her elbow. And when Eve clawed and tugged stubborn fleece to the shape of thread, Atra would nip at it too. At night, the lamb sprawled near Eve, her breathing warm and fragile, softening, at times, into dreaming sighs.

The lamb was with her, closer than Adam, when Eve's own labor began. When she drew her first sharp breath and clutched her belly, Atra quieted and pressed near, her expression close to frowning.

The pain spent as though it had never been, Eve smiled and resumed her work. She could perform it almost joyfully, now that it was so nearly finished. For God had said, had He not?—surely her memory couldn't falter here, in anything so vital—that her seed would crush the head of the serpent.

Then the disobedience and its consequences would be erased. She and Adam and God and the child would walk together through Eden. Her hands would once again be soft and smooth, and Adam would never frown. God would know that they could never again be enticed by a serpent. Or by anyone. And the child—

How was it, each time she thought of him, that her thoughts stumbled? That when she tried to picture him, her mind filled with fog? At first, she had thought it simply that she had never seen a human child; that there had never been a human child to see! But one night she had dreamed. And it was not a child she saw, but a man full-grown, enveloped in glory, as God had been. In her dream, she had shaded her eyes, and she had eased to her knees in worship, even knowing that she, the Mother of all living, must also be the mother of this Man, unless . . .

She had thought that it might be God Himself. There was much there, in addition to the light, that was of God. There was an expression at once of power and of gentleness.

She had been wakened from that dream—that vision?—by the heavy beating of her son's small feet within her.

Another small pain brought a gasp of surprise.

Soon, so very soon, God's promise would be visible! Her heart surged with expectation. Then she remembered Kara, and excitement dimmed.

At midday, when Adam returned from the fields, he was silent. Unapproachable. He ate broodingly, his glance on nothing within vision.

Eve had learned, at such times, to be silent, too.

She felt only one contraction during the meal, and hid that by bending with it, by pretending to retrieve a fallen grinding-stone.

He threw her a small glance of annoyance, then continued chewing contemplatively. The yearning for him to be close to her was strong, but a strain of pride prohibited her speaking.

The labor of animals began quietly, she knew, with unrest and small discomforts, and so might hers. There was, perhaps, time enough for Adam to find in the fields a healing for his mood.

All afternoon she worked at small things—filling the waterskins, tidying the shelter, cleansing the knife Adam had fashioned from ores melted and poured into a mold he'd shaped in mud. If human young were fastened like lambs in the womb of the ewe, would he use that to cut the cord?

She sighed.

Never had she felt so keenly her lack of background, of companionship. Of someone who had walked this path before, who could warn and comfort her.

Even Adam, had he been there, could only have held her.

That could have been enough.

By midafternoon, the sun beginning to decline, the pains were closer. And sharper, though still bearable.

Atra lay huddled in a spot of shadow, her eyes troubled. Occasionally, when Eve gasped with sharp surprise, the lamb lifted her head, bleating querulously.

You care, Eve thought. *At least* you *care.* And her glance sought Adam— now bending to a row of melons, now prodding the hoof of a limping ram, now securing a drooping olive limb, now carrying wood. Never, it seemed, looking her way.

Why is he angry with me? she wondered, retracing the events of the morning for some forgotten word, which might have wounded.

Perhaps he grieved again for Eden. Perhaps she took for anger what was merely sorrow.

As she felt sorrow now, for pain experienced, for pain anticipated.

"In sorrow you shall bring forth children," God had promised.

A new pain struck her, and she bent with it; tears sparked her eyes.

"For someone who traded a perfectly sound rib for a helper," Adam said sourly from the far side of the shelter, "I seem to be working alone a great deal."

She compressed her lips, fighting back softness. "Perhaps *you'd* like to take a turn carrying our child," she offered stiffly. "What is it you need?"

"We lost three ewes last night." His voice betrayed weariness and defeat. Compassion supplanted her anger and self-pity. "Oh, Adam. I'm sorry."

"And well you should be. Three ewes less to drop their young, this year and next—and next. Less wool, less meat, less everything."

She knew that the tightness in his voice was not really anger at her, though he might think so. "How?" she asked.

"What does it matter how? If they'd fallen from a cliff, they'd be as dead. Or if they'd drowned. Or eaten poison weeds."

"Wolves, then?" she prodded gently.

He struck his hand to the table. "Woman, you prattle endlessly! Could you still your tongue and be of some use to me?"

She blinked back tears. "What would you have me do?" Her knees weakened with a stronger pain, but she suppressed it.

"I've cut the posts for fencing. I need some vine. Enough to keep the sheep enclosed at night. Here. Close to us."

She inclined her head and, clutching the knife, moved toward the grove where vines grew thick and ancient, looping from tree to tree.

These were too high for her to reach, and her child throbbed lower in her body as she braced her foot against a leaning trunk and tried to raise herself.

Deep in the woods, the vines were more accessible.

Blinded by tears, she moved that way. Her sandals slapped determinedly; her thoughts churned. When he knew, he'd be sorry. He'd beg her forgiveness, and she might—she *might* give it sweetly, compounding his guilt. Or she might turn away—

Suddenly, he was beside her. "You were right." His hands dropped to her belly, gently. "Carrying our child is work enough."

How could she stay angry with him when that gentle smile lit his eyes with tenderness?

She couldn't. She pressed her hands to his chest and leaned against him. "Not for much longer," she whispered, and tears drizzled down her cheeks. They were not, as God had suggested, *all* tears of sorrow.

His hands caught her shoulders. *"Now? Today?"*

She nodded against him.

Another pain. Twisting. Wracking. What a relief to have him share it!

"Should I carry you?"

She giggled.

"I *could,*" he insisted, and she thought, *So like a little boy.* But how could she know that? Still, something within her reinforced the whimsy. This child—this son she was so soon to bear—might one day speak in just that way, pushing his chest far out to make himself seem taller.

"Of course you could." They turned together, walking slowly. "And who'd rub your back for you? Besides, you need your strength."

Another pain!

"We both do."

At the last—in the tearing, searing, screaming agony of it—she felt a soul-closeness with Kara.

And God had said that her *conceptions* would be multiplied, that she would bear her *children* in sorrow.

How many? she wondered. *How often?* Would each time be so dreadful?

Beneath, within, around it all wound Adam's dear voice, now tender, now soothing, now raw with anguish and strained with fear. If she were to die, what would he do, alone? Surely, she was dying. Surely, no fragile framework of bone and tissue could long endure such wracking.

Shards of disturbing memory disrupted the hours of labor with vivid images. She and Adam waiting in Eden, hidden from God . . . when without warning an eagle turned from feeding berry seed to her fledgling and plummeted to earth, talons extended, spearing a field mouse . . . blood smearing the vicious curve of bone . . . and a lioness suddenly turned from grazing to fell and gut a young gazelle . . .

And her silent screaming, echoing within her, battering at each nerve ending, needing the release of sound—except that God might hear and find them.

Had it happened, really? Or had the images generated within her mind? One day, she'd ask Adam.

"Adam?"

"I'm here."

"Do you remember—" A new contraction mangled speech and spirit.

"Don't talk just now. We'll talk later."

"Later," she sighed.

And there had been the slaughter of animals to shape their clothing. And in God's eyes, she had seen the death of trust.

"I'm sorry. I'm sorry. I'm sorry. I'm sorry."

"Please, my sweet dear. There's nothing to be sorry for."

Of course there was. If only God could realize how deeply she regretted—

Another pain. Another. And another, until she seemed to be a volcano, heaving and contracting with explosions of pain. Writhing with pain. Absorbed by pain, by pain, by pain, by pain—

"He's *here!* I see his head!"

She pushed. She could do nothing *but* push.

"His shoulders, now."

The *agony!* Excruciating. Vibrant.

She panted. *Poor Kara,* she thought, and whispered, "Kara . . ."

Another pain, another push, and a sweet, consuming emptiness of feeling.

"My son," Adam was saying, and she could feel his turning from her. "God has given me a son!"

I had some tiny part in it, my love, she thought.

But she said only, "I have gotten a man from the Lord." *As He promised,* she continued, only in her thoughts. Then she whispered, "Please, Adam . . . please. Please let me hold our son."

Three

Fanning herself with a broad leaf, Eve rested within the shelter and watched Cain.

He was a sturdy, beautiful son, alert and quick. She prayed that the second child, already moving lazily within her womb, would be as healthy and handsome.

Adam's bright hair curled on Cain's tiny scalp. Her own eyes, deep-fringed and hazel, looked back at her with a range of moods she had yet to master.

"His willfulness," Adam often said. "If only we can curb his willfulness."

Cain toddled, playing with Atra's most recent lamb, while Atra—a matron, now, and dignified—watched from a distance.

Content, Eve reached for fleece and spindle. She worked absently, her mind on Adam. He gathered grapes that day, far from her sight but never from her thoughts.

Adam.

How they had changed, the two of them, even in the past two years. How they'd grown from knowing Cain. From learning his care. From watching him learn.

Had God changed similarly, she wondered, as He'd watched them frolic through Eden? Had He felt that warm yearning in His loins—a need that they never feel pain or sorrow—as she experienced it for Cain? Had He known that surge of pride, straightening His limbs and shoulders, when they accomplished and discovered, as she and Adam had expanded at Cain's first gurgles, his tentative first steps? Had He laughed tenderly, protectively, as they played tag, or giggled foolishly?

Deliberately, she broke off both thread and thought.

Inevitably, such thinking led to the serpent.

She shuddered. Atra, perhaps sensing the shifting climate of her mood, bleated an anxious question, but never moved from her chosen spot.

"It's all right," Eve called softly. *It is good,* she finished in her thoughts.

Strange how those words—God's sentence of completion, of approval—wound through their lives. In Eden, it had paced the happy pitch of every moment—until that day. All had been good, happy, replete.

But since—

There lay surprise. That even *since* God's anger and their shame, much had been good.

Much still was good.

And much—she was certain—*much would be good.* For God had promised that her seed . . .

Cain's high chortle broke into her thoughts. She watched as he held the lamb (small, fat fingers wound through fleece) and tried to mount. The lamb jiggled and bucked, but Cain was determined. No longer chortling, his jaw set firmly, he swung one short fat leg across the shaggy back.

Both lamb and boy collapsed in rising dust.

Before the clouds had settled, the struggle renewed.

Eve smiled. The thread, harsh against her calloused fingers, was firm and reassuring. *Like the fabric of our lives,* she thought, *the elements in each of us contributing a safe predictability toward each day.*

Oh, there were variations in their moods. There were moments when Adam and she struck sparks, igniting quarrels. But they always passed, their tension easing once again to the comfortable rhythms of sameness.

And Cain.

Cain was determined, sometimes sunny, often helpful. Or so he thought. But there were times when fever's warmth or some small injury brought lassitude and whining, and her quick fear. Then she would hug him tensely. She could not bear to lose him! Not him; not Adam. She had already lost so much. Eden. And Kara. She could not, *would* not, lose more.

Though of course she would. *They* would.

Each year, as seasons changed, they lost. Spring's delicacy died to summer's bounty, which died to harvest, which died to winter's fallow time. Each change a loss—or growth? A step in climbing? Perhaps a trade for something better, as Adam's trade of rib for wife—she hoped—had bettered him.

Since winter led to spring again, and each year's growth seemed stronger, each harvest broadening, surely the gain was greater than the loss.

In harvests and in seasons, she could sense the pattern.

Surely, it shaped their lives, as well. There had been moments when she'd caught its essence—freshening, enriching, then escaping, unreclaimable.

Once she had thought, on waking, that God had never meant for them to stay long in Eden. That perhaps He'd planted, deep within them, that tiny seed of disobedience, *wanting* them to sin, to be expelled from perfect peace. To struggle toward something greater than eternal childlikeness.

But she had squelched that thought, denying it.

Now, unguarded, she toyed with the thought again. Within her stirred a knowledge that Adam would be angry if he knew, and would rail at her. That God would surely know, and . . . what? How could He punish her more thoroughly than He'd already done?

And instantly, she realized. He could take Cain. Or Adam.

She dropped both yarn and spindle, deserting shade, and hurried to the heat.

Atra, bleating, rose from her comfort and came running, her hooves a heavy pattering, where once they'd been like beetles, clicking on a table. Cain, also apparently alarmed, relaxed his fingerholds of fleece and the lamb scampered away, bleating triumph.

Cain wailed, and Eve considered comfort, but walked instead toward the willow-bordered stream for ease of her own spirit.

Cain would be fine. Once his frustration had been voiced, he'd sober and catch the lamb again. Before the day was over, he'd have his way.

He always did.

Adam turned from the spring, where he washed a huge cluster of grapes. He held it high for her to see. "As fine as any in Eden!" he exclaimed, and offered it to her with tender ceremony.

"Oh, Adam," she breathed.

"I know," he said, and held her close, the smell of his sweat both vibrant and immensely comforting. "I love you, too."

But would he love her still, she wondered, if he could guess the errant path her thoughts so often took? If he could know her questioning, her throbbing, deep uncertainties? And, worst of all, the questionable answers she'd begun to frame?

During long evenings, as Cain slept sweetly on his pallet and the sheep stirred and murmured in the corral, Eve loved to watch the silver etchings of moonlight shifting with nature's movements.

There, foliage stirred, forming new spots and splashes. And there, some animal strayed past the rigid line of shadow, shaping new patterns.

It was the variety of night she loved the most. The unexpectedness. Beauty and anguish, juxtaposed. Softness and ruggedness meeting.

And the expectation.

Night was *filled* with expectation. With dreams of Cain's growing. The coming of the second child.

"If it should be a girl this time," Adam asked one evening, while the baby rippled under his quiet hand, "will you name her Kara?"

"Kara," she repeated gently. She wondered if the ewe could possibly have been so important for so long if she had lived.

"You mentioned her name, when Cain was born."

"I was thinking of her. The way she died. I felt that *I* would die."

His touch hardened—then, as though with conscious effort, fell away.

There followed a long beat of silence. But it was soft, warm silence, the sharing continued.

"Would it be fitting?" she asked.

"Whatever you like would be . . . fitting."

She heard the smiling in his words, and she smiled, too. "You're the best with naming, after all. What would you choose?"

He was quiet in that way he had when thoughts ran deep. "I'd have to see her first, I think."

"If she has tight-curled hair, like fleece, and pale, like fleece . . ."

"We'll call her Kara!"

They laughed together, gently.

He caught her hand. More silence followed.

"Eve?"

"Hmmmm?"

There was no warning that this conversation could be the one so carefully avoided for so long.

"Do you ever miss . . . everything?"

Everything, she thought.

Eden.

"Yes." She paused. "Don't you?"

"Of course. And yet—"

She understood.

"There's something about"—he paused—"the *struggle.*"

"I know." Her spirit throbbed. He sensed it, too, this *rightness* she so often felt.

His voice was very young as he said, "Today I found a way to dam the stream."

"*Really!*" The word was warm with praise, and he stirred beside her. "And the animals?"

"Won't break it, I believe." Another pause. "We'll know tomorrow."

"And if they have, in some way, broken it?"

"We'll find another way." His voice was quiet with confidence.

She turned her mind to images of Eden. There he had tended vines that never failed, and planted shoots that always grew.

"And yet there are times." His voice vibrated with loss. "I remember Him, walking so close."

She covered his hand with hers, but, carefully, he freed himself. Loss twisted within her.

"He was my *friend!*" he said intensely.

She didn't speak. She had no right to.

"He's out there, somewhere. I feel it, often—especially like this, at night. When there were just the two of us, we walked at night, and He taught me—" His voice fractured. "I can't remember some of it. When we were forced to leave, it left me."

She hugged herself against an inner chill. *When we were forced to leave.*

How often she'd submerged that memory. Some day, when she was strong, she'd have to face it. Not now. Not with the baby surging within her.

So soon the child would come. She wondered if the pain would be as devastating as with Cain. If she could be so frightened. If Adam would.

Realizing what would be involved could make it easier to face. Or harder.

"If it's a boy," suggested Adam, his hand on hers again, his voice once more his own, "I'd like to name him Abel."

They had woven a basket of reeds for Abel, and it hung from the tent brace, swinging its rounded bottom just inches from the mats. Adam had completed the tent just days before the birth—with Cain chattering in broken phrases, delivered at excitement's pitch, as he "helped."

The abandoned shelter would be used for cooking, for necessary tool repair, for preparation of the wool for spinning.

Eve had devised a method, setting her spindle in a leather brace, from which the thread spun with greater evenness, much faster than before. And she had learned—by weaving the threads from side to side, through vertical yarns impaled on thorns—to fashion cloth more comfortable for children's clothing than were the heavy skins. Sometimes Adam lifted a swatch of this cloth, holding it toward the light, allowing it to float upon his hand. "When you have time—" he'd venture, and she'd smile, imagining the garments she'd one day make for him. And for herself.

For the first weeks following delivery, while Cain and Adam worked at various tasks, Eve stayed in the tent or near it, caring for Abel. But once he'd settled and her strength returned, Adam carried the basket with them, fastening it to some close tree for shade and safety, while they worked together in the fields or growing vineyards.

"Cain," Eve called one day.

Cain pulled a weed, then, squatting, caught another.

"Cain!"

His stiffened shoulders and studied nonchalance proved that he'd heard her. Yet he patted the soil around the tiny plants and moved ahead without a word.

"*Cain!*" Adam's tone was stern, and Cain rose slowly, turning. He stood, his small head bowed, hands grimy at his sides. "Your mother called you."

Cain feigned surprise.

"When your mother calls, you answer."

He nodded, sighing. "Yes, my father."

Lashes still lowered, Cain flicked a glance toward Eve. She saw it. And he must surely know that she had seen. Yet, determinedly, he bent once more to his row.

Eve felt an apprehension out of all proportion to Cain's defiance. Just for an instant, she'd remembered the eyes of the serpent. His independence. His arrogance.

She shuddered, willing the thought away. Cain, *her seed,* had nothing save a shared enmity in common with the serpent. God had promised.

Cain, small shoulders set and stubborn, moved to other plants.

Eve swung the cradle absently, considering alternatives. She could ignore Cain's willfulness and simply go about her work. Then, when Abel cried, she could insist that Cain obey. Still, he'd have stored within his mind the victory already won, and gain incentive for rebellions later.

She might approach him unobtrusively and take his arm, forcing him to his task. But he might use the fragile basket roughly, from his anger.

She could, of course, let Adam handle it. Yet how she dreaded any application of a switch to that small, rounded rump. Still, if Cain feared it, why did he provoke it? Perhaps he didn't mind at all, but sensed how she did.

In the end, she broke the switch herself, and swung it, casually, watching to catch his glance.

Small hands moved slowly, weed to weed. Then, pretending to chase a gnat, Cain caught her glance, and smiled. "Mother," he called, his voice bright and alert, "could I rock Abel for you?"

Caught off-guard, she simply handed him the switch—for chasing flies.

Adam threw his son a pleased, proud look.

Quietly, they worked through the humming heat of morning, while Eve considered Cain. He knew so much—so soon!—of subtlety.

And Abel. What elements would Abel bring to stir into the medley of their lives?

Sighing, she shut her mind to wondering.

The weeds, at least, though bothersome, knew nothing of intrigue.

"It's time," Adam announced one Seventh Day. He and Eve sat on sun-warmed rocks, while Cain counted daisies and Abel slept in his almost-outgrown basket, set in shaded grass. "It's time we think about the future."

She would have laughed, but for his seriousness. What could they guess of "future"? How could they plan for it?

"When I was in the Garden—" He broke off, perhaps sensing her possible reaction to the singular. "Before God gave you to me—" He cleared his throat. "He told me, many times, just how He'd shaped the world and all that's in it." He prodded a tree-toad with a blade of grass, and the small creature shifted lazily, then settled, squat again. "How each part happened, day by day. And in what order." He glanced at her, a furrow between his brows.

"Yes," she prompted gently. "I remember."

"In the beginning, God created the heaven and the earth. . . ."

She picked up the flow of melodious narrative, joining him. "And the earth was without form, and void; and darkness was upon the face of the deep."

"And the Spirit of God moved upon the"—he hesitated, then continued— "upon the face of the waters."

It's beautiful, she thought. The words flowed like deep water over sparkling pebbles, quiet and strong and reassuring. There was in them that kind of peace induced by branches waving in a gentle breeze, the quiet grandeur of massive clouds embracing distant mountain peaks.

"It must never be forgotten," Adam said. "When Cain is old—and Abel— they must remind their children, and when their children's children's children are old, they must still remember. Remember, and pass it on."

The thought swelled within her, bringing excitement and a vision of unnumbered crowds of men and women, boys and girls, filling the earth, chanting the rhythms, which told so glowingly of God's creation. Had God not said that she would be the mother of all living? And so her blood must flow in all their veins.

A touch of pride flavored her thoughts.

She and Adam would be honored. Revered. Those hordes of people would look to them for wisdom. For advice. For experience. Adam could show the men how he had wrested rock from the earth and made it metal. And she could demonstrate the alchemy of sheep fleece turned to cloth, and flax to thread. And when the women's bellies stretched and strained with children, she would advise and comfort, giving encouragement. Assurance. Gentling them through the fiercest pangs by telling them that once the pain was past, once they held their children, the agony might never have been.

And what will you tell them, something asked within her, *when they wonder why such things must be at all? Why they no longer live at ease, in perfect happiness, in Eden?*

She wondered if that might be God, within her, nudging her toward honesty. Humility.

She squirmed on the warm rock. Her mind returned to present things, to Adam, softly whispering some later phrases from God's record of creation, ". . . And the evening and the morning were the first day."

All that in one day, she thought, her heart stirring with praise. To take the nothingness and give it form. To shape and name the light and darkness—all in a single day! It had taken Adam weeks to realize how fire could be started, and they were still discovering new ways to use it.

God had not discovered anything, but *made* it—designed, devised, and *made* it—all in a slender span of days.

"Adam."

She had interrupted the flow of the poem, and he seemed to hold it in some spot of memory before he fully released his attention to her.

"How can we teach them? How can we *know* they'll remember?" *Or that we will,* she finished, but only in her mind. So often, things slipped through the mesh of her memory, never to be recovered.

His eyes widened. "I could never forget," he said with quiet assurance. "But—" His glance strayed to Cain.

Still counting daisies, Eve noticed. How could he bear to spend all of his time with plants? He had early lost interest in the animals, hated even to help his father chase the sheep into the safety of the corral at evening, and shunned the cackling fowls and their flapping wings. It was with the greatest reluctance that he would gather eggs. Eve was certain that he feared the larger animals, the oxen, especially. For smaller animals, like toads and frogs, he had some interest. She'd seen him watch a chameleon for hours, moving it from one place to another, to force its changing camouflage. But for those animals that had some value, and with which he'd have to learn to work as he grew older, he had disdain, at best.

She realized, suddenly, that Adam had been answering her question.

"—each night," he was saying. "Like a tool etching into a stone, the lines will deepen into ruts of memory, so that nothing can erase them."

Each night, she thought, scrambling to reclaim what must have gone before. Each night . . . to repeat the whole record of creation? To say it over and over and over, Cain saying it, too, and eventually Abel. *And,* she thought secretly, not having mentioned it to Adam yet, still uncertain, *that other child, still small within?* (A bud; no more than that. A whisper.) To have them—all of them, however many that might be, in time—repeat the rhythmic lines each night . . .

She imagined it beside the fire. The sparks, forming new, fragile stars above them. They would sit in a circle, perhaps, and chant the words. And the words might be a sweet fragrance, rising to God Himself, pleasing Him.

They began that very night, Adam drawing Cain into his arms and explaining. Cain was quiet, at first, savoring the attention, Eve was sure, and perhaps sensing some seriousness from Adam's tone. He listened quietly, through the earlier stanzas, then nodded off.

Adam and Eve, though, finished the poem before taking the children to bed.

In bed themselves, later, the night fire burning brightly, casting intermittent patterns of light against the tent, Eve sighed with contentment.

Adam, too, seemed at peace.

And Eve felt sure that wherever God walked that night, alone, He, too, was pleased.

The nightly ritual added new dimension to their lives.

Eve felt her spirits lifting, calming, as each evening meal was cleared and Adam set about the feeding and corraling. She could see peace written on his features, too. And an expectancy.

Abel, too young to understand, would sit on Eve's knee during the recital. But sometimes even he would be involved, cooing and swinging tiny hands in rhythm with the lines. Should Adam notice, smiling around the words he repeated, Cain would, in some way, unfailingly reclaim his attention.

Little Deri, dark-haired and even-tempered, slept in the basket. Deep within her, Eve was sure, another small life stirred.

At first, Cain had been unable to remain awake throughout the whole poem. Later, he'd begun to question portions of it. "Why did God call the water *seas,* Father? Why didn't He wait and have you name them?" Or, "Why did He make the plants first and *then* the animals? 'Cause the plants were more important?"

Once Adam had answered each question carefully and deeply, Cain would settle back in happy concentration. Most recently, he'd begun to chime in with bits and pieces he remembered from the litany.

"I'm pleased," Adam confided, more than once. "Only if he knows it thoroughly himself can he teach others."

At Palie's birth, a new tradition surfaced.

"God has enriched us," Adam said, "first with two sons to help me in the fields, and now with two daughters—who will someday bear sons of their own."

"Or bear daughters?" Eve asked, with forced lightness. Still, a residue of resentment clung, and his startled glance and swift color testified that he had caught it.

"I'm . . . I wasn't thinking," he stammered, catching her close and continuing miserably. "You *know* how I love them, and my love for you—" He choked back a sob, and she found herself patting, consoling, comforting.

Of course he loved them—her and their daughters! And it wasn't Adam who had commanded her subservience.

But surely for Deri, crawling and chortling in the wake of a duckling, and for Palie, and for all those other daughters who would spin and weave and dream and cook and love their families—surely God's punishment would wane, and they could someday walk on equal footing with their men, as she herself had, while in Eden.

Adam had regained his composure. "They are *all* strong children, healthy and bright. For them, and for you, my dear"—his glance touched her with such warmth that she felt a flaming in her cheeks—"I thank God nightly."

"Adam," she murmured, and bowed her head. Within, joy bloomed. Each night, he thanked their God for her . . . as she thanked Him for Adam.

She'd never been certain that God heard her thanks, and even less that He'd accept them. There was no voice, as there had been in Eden. No sight of Him, nor sound of His stirring. Still, once she'd thanked Him, she always knew a peace. A rightness.

She wondered if it seemed like that for Adam, after he'd prayed.

"—and so today," he finished—and she wondered what she'd lost, between—"today, I'll choose a kid. Best of the flock, without a blemish. And Cain will help me!"

Despite his usual reticence in tending animals, Cain seemed infected by his father's enthusiasm. He began a strange hopping routine, on one foot, then the other, then both, and chanted in sing-song fashion, "I get to he-elp! A-bel doesn't!"

Abel began to cry.

Deri, in sympathy, abandoned the ducklings, plopped into the dust, and began a mournful wailing of her own.

And Palie, too young to take sides, puckered her infant mouth and joined the chorus.

"Oh, Cain," Eve murmured. "Why must you always—"

"I wan' to helllllp!" cried Abel.

It wrenched Eve's heart. He was such a sunny child, except when Cain tormented him.

Adam swept Abel into his arms. "Then help you shall!" he shouted, spinning about until both were reeling and laughing.

Lifting Palie from her cradle, Eve glanced at Cain. He was standing very still, his shoulders slumping, his lower jaw jutting, the image of total desolation.

She thought of asking that Abel stay with her, helping to crack almonds, a task he loved.

But Adam, Abel astride his shoulders, was out of easy hearing distance.

"Cain," she suggested gently, and nodded after them.

He hesitated.

She knew precisely what he needed: for Adam to remember that he stood there. To wait, to call for him. To give him just the kind of individual love and attention Cain himself had caused to go to Abel.

With Palie in her arms, she bent to him. "He loves you, son," she reassured him gently. "And he needs your help. Now, see—he's nearly out of sight!"

The words must have been right. He dashed at his eyes with his fist, summoned a straggly smile, pecked her cheek quickly, and ran off yelling, "I'm coming! Wait! Wait for me!"

Softly, Eve touched her cheek. It had been her first unsolicited kiss from Cain in a long time. Abel was always showing love. Deri was gluttonous for hugs and kisses.

But Cain was a strange one. There were times she feared for him. And times she thought she couldn't bear another minute of his moods and mischief. And times when she was sadly certain that it could not be Cain who would fulfill God's promise.

Not Cain. Perhaps Abel, then? She sighed, afraid to hope too strenuously.

Palie was nursing, and Deri down for her nap, when they returned. Adam still carried Abel—also half-asleep—and Cain half-carried, half-dragged the kid. A perfect white one, impatient with his captor.

The child was nearly spent, Eve noticed. Gasping, he laid himself full-length across the kid's back, as though to pinion it until he was capable of further struggle.

"Adam," she said, almost reprovingly.

"He insisted," said Adam, easing Abel to his pallet. He settled beside Eve, touching his forefinger to Palie's soft cheek, then—just a thumbnail's length away—to Eve's breast. "Both softer than lambskin," he murmured, and returned his attention to Cain.

"That might be a good place for him right there, son," he said. "Could you hold him just a bit longer, until I get the rope and peg?"

Gasping for breath, Cain nodded gratefully.

Once the kid was tethered and Cain recovered, he asked, "Why did you stake him there, Father? Why not put him with the others?"

"Because," said Adam, "he's not *like* the others." He dropped to a knee beside the child. "Remember how careful we were in choosing him?"

Cain nodded.

"Remember who I told you the kid was for?"

Cain frowned, saying tentatively, "You *said* for God."

Listening, Eve caught her breath. So that was what she'd missed earlier, while her thoughts strayed.

"That's right, son. For God. When we give gifts, we want them to be perfect. Remember the whistle I carved for you?"

Cain nodded. "It wasn't perfect, though. One note—"

Adam's laughter cut short his words. "As perfect as possible, then," he said, ruffling the child's bright hair. "I'm not a maker of perfect whistles, I'm afraid. But," his voice grew serious, "I *am* a herder of perfect sheep and goats. At least, some of them are perfect. And the most perfect"—he touched the kid's sleek back—"the most perfect must be our gift to God."

Cain knelt. His finger traced around the kid's eye. "God will like him."

Softly, "I hope so, son."

"When will He come for him, Father? And will I see Him?"

Palie had finished nursing, her mouth grown slack around the oozing nipple. Adjusting her robe, Eve carried the babe to her basket again. When she returned, the conversation had taken a frighteningly different turn.

Cain was standing rigid, his face contorted, his fists clenched and active. "You mean you're goin' t' *burn* him? You're goin' t' burn this perfect little kid I helped you find? But how can you *do* that? How can God *want* that! I wish I'd helped him run away, instead of—" Eyes streaming, he gave Adam one last unbelieving look and ran sobbing toward the stream.

Later, Cain helped to build the altar. But there was no joy in his work. Abel carried tiny stones, one at a time, and waited with each one for Adam's thanks and recognition, but Cain worked doggedly, his small face pale and joyless.

When the altar was ready, when Adam had cleansed both himself and the kid, he laid the small animal on the kindling. With solemn ceremony, he slit its throat.

Cain gave a strangled cry and turned away, and Eve moved to comfort him. She was shaken herself, reminded uncomfortably of the animals killed to make their first clothing. She felt her hands tremble on his frail shoulders.

But then she listened to Adam's voice, offering vibrant thanks to God for all their children, all their blessings. And she caught the fragrance of the smoke, and watched it billow upward.

"Look," she urged Cain, gently. "Not at the altar, at the sky."

Obediently, he lifted his eyes, following the rising smoke.

"It's the kid," she said. "Your father's sending it to God."

He stared at her, unbelieving.

"Yes!" she insisted. "God couldn't come to us"—*or wouldn't,* she finished in her thoughts—"and so your father's sending it the only way he knows."

Cain's eyes were downcast again. "He *killed* it," he argued sullenly.

"I know." She paused, not knowing what to add. She didn't quite understand herself why such a gift, a gift of death, should be pleasing to the God who'd created all of life.

Then, suddenly, forming from the billows of smoke, was the shape of a kid. A perfect kid. "Oh, look! Cain, *look!*" One moment it remained identifiable, and then it might have represented anything. Or nothing.

One moment was enough.

Cain pulled away, gently, his head tilting back as the shapeless smoke ascended. Then he turned glowing eyes toward Eve's face. "He really did," he said softly. "He really *did* send the little kid to God!"

The altar remained, a monument to what had happened there, although the stones were clean of ashes, and nearly bare of smudges. Eve walked that way, early one morning, before the children wakened. No sign of blood. Or bone. The fire had licked it clean—carrying it whole to God?

Eve felt a gnawing sense of loss, sharp and vivid.

In Eden, there had been no sacrifice—save, following their sin, the death of innocent animals to mask newly discovered nakedness.

In Eden, praise and thanksgiving would have been offered directly. Simply. Face to face. And God would have answered.

She'd heard no answer to this sacrifice of Adam's.

Dew lay thick upon the grass and fields. She stooped to touch a spray of pea vine, its vivid green hazed with health, and remembered how, just a few short years ago, she had grieved for their endless labor in the fields.

The work was hard, still. They "ate their bread in the sweat of their faces." Nothing came easily. Unless they tilled the ground and cared for the trees and tended the flocks, there would be no food.

Nothing had changed in that direction.

But *she* had changed. (Had Adam? She thought so.) She no longer felt the panic. The acute abandonment. The anger and betrayal.

All that had been replaced by . . . a sense of justice? A sense of purpose. And fulfillment.

Having the children helped. They were the future, as well as enrichment for the present. Each was a unique reason for the struggle. A daily joy, as well as challenge. A growing gift from God, who still, perhaps, remembered them with love.

Four

As the rich weeks passed, paced by nature's rhythms, the fields were tilled, planted, tended, harvested.

And each succeeding harvest was more plentiful. More pleasing.

Oat straw, stacked loosely in late summer, gleamed golden in autumn's sunglow. Fruit, freshly picked and gathered into sacks, spread a vivid fragrance over a landscape already ornate with the vibrant hues of foliage and flowers and dying grasses. In the shelter near the tent lay heaped sacks bulky with dried vegetables or heavy with oats, wheat, and barley.

And, within Eve's womb, a fifth child grew toward a different type of harvest.

"God has blessed our toil," said Adam. For Eve, his words wore the rhythm and beauty of another litany. "He has noted the troubles that afflict us, and has given increase. He has subdued the ground, for our sakes, and has given us the victory over thorns and thistles. He sends the dew each night, that the earth might not withhold its bounty. He fattens within the womb the young of our herds." His voice deepened with increased emotion as he added, "And, in the womb of the woman He gave me, He grants continued blessings."

Eve's heart stirred with the rich phrases. A song, she thought. A hymn of praise. Like the psalm of creation—recited so often that it frequently rose, whole and unbidden, to her thoughts—Adam's hymn spoke from and to the spirit.

"It is time," he said, "that we make another sacrifice to show our gratitude." His glance touched Cain, but the flicker of uncertainty passed from his eyes in a moment. "It is only right that we do this. It pleases God."

Eve threw him a quick, hard look, but he had turned away.

He had spoken with such certainty! How did he know what pleased God? Had God spoken to him? She felt a pang of jealousy. Had they been meeting secretly—shutting her out as an extension of her punishment, greater than Adam's because hers had been the greater sin?

Or *had* it?

She had been tempted by the serpent. She still remembered his beauty, the glow, which had enveloped him, the hypnotic movement of his sinews, and the subtlety with which he'd spoken. While she had fallen prey to the polish and sophistication of such a creature, Adam had been tempted merely by her. Even considering his love for her, whose was the greater failing?

Yet Adam had excused himself by emphasizing her blame.

When the children ran to her with tales about one another, or tried to shift blame, she scolded them. But Adam—perhaps because he'd been fresh from the hand of God, and she shaped (a bit more casually?) only from rib—Adam had come away from the painful interview punished and chastened, surely, but not as severely as she.

Still, could God err?

Could the actual events of that day have blurred in memory? Carefully, she'd held at bay remembrance of those painful scenes: God's finding them, His anger, their expulsion.

Perhaps now was the time to face the memories honestly, recalling each dreadful detail, however searing to her senses. Perhaps only after she had done that could she conquer her recurring questions about God. About God and herself. About herself and Adam.

What *had* happened that terrible day . . . ?

Even above the roaring of the waterfall, they'd heard His footsteps.

The ground shook with their pressure, and the sky seemed riven with sound and light. Birds rose from their branches, shrieking. The lioness, licking the naked bones of the young gazelle, while her cubs drowsed near her, stiffened in fear and hurried her stumbling family ahead of her, out of sight. Out of danger.

The woman's breath tore at her lungs. Instinctively, she clung to Adam; they clung to one another. Intuitively, they shrank behind their barrier of shrubbery. She yearned for the ground to open and enclose them in its darkness. Anything. Anything to escape—

"*Adam!*" He called. His voice was everywhere. Trees quivered. A rock at the rim of the waterfall creaked and loosened, groaned, wavered, and tumbled—from ledge to ledge to ledge—crashing at last in rubble at the base.

"Adam! Where are you?"

There was no use, she knew. Adam would have to answer. She pulled slightly away, expecting him to stand and leave her crouching. Instead, he drew her toward him.

She had never fully noticed, before, the cocoon of brightness encasing God. She shielded her eyes against it, peering beneath her hand to distinguish those features she had known with such familiarity. But the brightness assaulted her.

Haltingly, Adam explained why they had hidden. Rather, why *he* had hidden. She wondered if God might ask her separately. Nervously, she cleared her throat in preparation.

But God's next question startled her. "Who told you that you were naked?" Through her confusion (because, of course, no one had *told* them; they'd just known) she heard Him answer with another question. Her confusion cleared to certainty.

He knew.

He knew where she'd been. What they had done. That they had disobeyed Him and eaten of the fruit of the forbidden tree. *How* had He known? Had the serpent told Him? Had He, perhaps, sent the serpent to test them?

But there was no time, then, for pursuing possibilities.

Adam's hand on her elbow was urging her before him. "The woman you gave me to be with me," he said, "gave me of the tree, and I did eat."

Anguished, tears starting to her eyes, she turned to stare at him, this man whose rib had become her, who had said they were one flesh, that he would hold only to her. This man who had shared her laughter and joy. This man she loved.

He wouldn't look at her. His eyes quivered in their sockets. His mouth was both tremulous and strained. His cheeks were stained with ugly, throbbing color.

Nothing God might have said, on finding them, could have cut her as deeply as Adam's denial of their oneness.

But now God *was* speaking to her, and she turned toward His light, flinching under the bombardment of His words, each inflicting injury and renewing shame.

And she answered as Adam had answered, with that same cowardice, blaming the serpent.

"Because you have done this," God began—and she looked up, thinking that He still spoke to her. But she gasped as she saw the serpent, who seemed shriveled before God, not poised or beautiful at all. As frightened and as shamed as she and Adam.

She felt Adam's arms encircling her, as though for mutual protection. Still stinging from his words, she would have liked to draw away. But she required that closeness, too.

Numbly, she heard God's curse upon the serpent. Part of her felt vindicated at his punishment, but another portion quailed—dreading that moment when God's anger turned, again, to Adam and to her.

Perhaps He wouldn't punish them further, beyond what they'd already suffered from their shame, their fear, the tremor of His steps, the volume of His voice.

Perhaps He'd called out more from worry than from anger, fearing them lost. Or injured. Or, knowing their sin, perhaps He'd thought them truly at fault, at first, until she'd told Him whose sin it really was. Now that He *knew*, now that His anger raged in cold, hard syllables over the serpent's head—

Now, surely, things could be as they'd been before.

But such an anger!

Adam's arm tightened about her. She could feel his quivering. She covered his hand with hers, communicating calmness, now that God's anger concentrated on the serpent.

Such harshness, she thought again, though no more than was deserved.

To be cursed above all the cattle of the field—he who had moved so proudly, who had been so skilled with words, who had been so persuasive and so beautiful. To crawl upon his belly—he who had moved with grace and eloquence. To eat the dust—he who had coiled so comfortably along the branches of the Tree of the Knowledge of Good and Evil.

To live in enmity with Woman.

That part God could have left unsaid, at least for her sake. Since the moment she and Adam had learned shame and fear, she'd hated the serpent. She always would. Each time she saw him she would strike him, hit him with sticks, crush him under stones, make him suffer.

Yet he looked so diminished now, so drained of beauty. So pathetic.

But God had returned His attention to *her*. In His voice she heard anger and sorrow commingled, and she knew that the ease she had felt in her mind had been a false security. He would not ignore her disobedience, whoever had occasioned it. Things would never, ever be the same again.

The pronouncements of punishment had been made.

She and Adam, chastened, stood with heads bowed as God fashioned their coats of skin. From the bodies of the animals, sleek and beautiful and trusting, had burst blood and other fluids, fat, bowels. Aliveness had been sacrificed to provide protection from the chill, which had already made the fig leaves seem inadequate.

Adam had named her Eve. Mother of all living.

The term meant nothing to her. There was no room in her mind for interpretation, for looking forward. All portions of her mind and heart yearned backward, to what could never be again.

Unless God changed His mind.

That seemed impossible.

Still sheathed in brightness, His features indistinguishable, there was a sorrow in His posture. In His tones, sensations of betrayal. A finality.

The God Who had created the light and the darkness and had pronounced them good, Who had fashioned every living thing with infinite attention to detail and found each good, Who had crowned His achievement with their creation and now found them wanting—that God was not about to bend from His decision.

Still, the touch of His hands as He clothed them was gentle.

Eve, tears blurring her eyes, her heart crying out to Him, leaned into that gentleness.

He stepped apart from them as He spoke His final words: "Behold, the Man is become as one of us, to know good and evil: and now, lest he put forth his hand and take also of the Tree of Life, and eat, and live forever—"

Was there, then, another tree—more important, even than the forbidden one? Had she and Adam ever passed it? Seen it? Even, lacking their present knowledge, tasted of its fruit?

Her mind trembled, reached out silently to God in pleading.

Surely, knowing what they knew now, they could be trusted. If God prohibited something, *any*thing, they could pass and shun it—not wanting, ever again, to feel this separation from Him. This space developing between the two of them. This anguish within.

You can trust us. She pushed the thought toward Him. *Please, please trust us.*

But she and Adam were being rushed along a path they'd never known before. A path dark and vine-entangled. Evil winds whispered among the dark trunks of twisted trees. Sharp stones turned beneath their feet. Brambles, reaching, snagged flesh and the fur of their garments, which still reeked of spilled blood. Strange lights more eerie than the darkness itself flickered here and there. A chill entered her bloodstream and curdled there. Soft screams spoke of weary terror. The cries of predators hung like vines in the air. Like serpents. Flames of red fire flickered and darted, wavered and extinguished, reappearing at such close range that they brought the stench of burning flesh, yet never decreased the cold.

Just where Eden ended, Eve was never certain. Just where the world-that-was-to-be-theirs began, she couldn't know. And if there were a corridor between the two, as she later suspected, she couldn't know its boundaries.

Days later, she left Adam tossing in his tortured sleep on the stony ground. A determination bred of her anguish and her guilt had been born within her.

She must try, one more time, to plead with God.

And so she turned back the way they had come, seeking Him.

But she hadn't gone far when she saw ahead of her a slender thread of flame, soaring skyward, cutting the darkness with slashes of vivid red and molten gold. Now flaring straight ahead of her, now turned to one side or the other, now interrupted by a looming, luminous figure.

How strange, she thought. How beautiful.

How frightening.

And then, when she'd drawn closer, she saw that the flame was a sword, sharp and powerful—and that the angel who held it blocked the only direction she knew to God. To Eden.

With a sense of shock, Eve returned from the stark chill of memory to the bright autumn plenty surrounding her.

So distant, that harsh expulsion from Eden, yet so close. So much a fabric of her very existence. The sheaves of straw remained as golden as before she'd summoned memory. The fragrance of the fruit as sweet and heavy on the warmth of late afternoon.

And yet she shivered, just a bit, from remembered cold—both of body and of spirit.

And her hatred of the serpent, agent of her temptation, ran fresh and strong through her fiber.

The children still played where she had left them when she'd departed in memory—however long ago that had been. Their sounds, though shrill, seemed compatible enough. And Adam had been close enough to monitor potential quarrels. He closed the sacks of new-threshed oats and wheat, pausing at times to run the grain between his fingers.

With the memory of pain and alienation so fresh, Eve doubted the contentment he communicated.

But if she walked for a time, alone—firming the corridor between past and present and cutting, surely forever, the cords that formed it—perhaps then she could reenter the world where Adam and the children smiled, and be a part of it again.

Eve felt fully at peace when she returned through lengthening shadows. She heard Palie's querulous voice and Abel's attempts at comfort. Adam was with the flocks, Deri beside him, hugging a lamb.

She didn't see Cain at first.

He might be working longer in the fields, enjoying the texture of anything green and growing—or brown and harvested, for that matter. Such an affinity he had for plants, that one!

She smiled, loving him in her mind.

He wasn't her favorite child. Each was her favorite in some small section of her heart, that spot determined by a certain need or trait of character.

For Abel, it was his sweet openness, his unrestrained outpouring of love to everyone. To everything. His quick understanding. His compassion.

With Deri, it was her bustling approach to homemaking. Not just to washing things, or shining them, or banishing dust—as much as it was possible to banish dust, where dust had governed long before they'd intervened. Deri cared for people, too, was concerned for their physical comfort. With emotions and other intangibles, however, she was as awkward as Abel was skilled.

Palie's delicacy spoke clearly to Eve. Her vulnerability. Her need for tenderness.

And Cain.

Cain's needs were perhaps the greatest. Beneath his carefully guarded exterior, Eve was convinced, he was as vulnerable as Palie. So inward, deep, and secretive. This child who caused her more concern than all the others, who held her distant—Cain, she was convinced, required a constant, patient love.

She finally found him in the flecked shadow of drying grapevines.

He was crooning, bent over something that moved in his arms.

The animal seemed longer than a toad, larger than any lizard she'd seen this side of Eden.

She moved toward him. And suddenly she knew.

He turned to her, his eyes elated, his smile becoming words: "See, Mother! See? I found him near the altar, and he lets me pet him—"

He shrank from her as she struck his arm, knocking the snake to the ground. His eyes darkened with fear.

It was a small snake, mottled green and gold (green like the verdant foliage of Eden; gold like the play of sunlight on her gentle waterfall). That it wasn't poisonous was evident in the sharpness of nose and tail. But its eyes glistened. And as she watched its forked tongue flick in red, hypnotic rhythms, as its coils formed and moved, grief renewed, fresh from her recent musings. Fresh from memories so long submerged that their vividness now would have frightened her, had she been rational.

But she was not rational. And her freshly honed anguish, needing some focus other than her own sin of disobedience, centered on the small, hapless reptile.

"You!" she said, and her voice rose to a shriek. "*You!*" She brought her sandaled heel to its head once, twice. "You robbed us of Eden—" another thump of her heel, and she felt something crack. "You robbed usss of God!" It still moved. Blindly, she fumbled for a stone and found one, plying it with awkward viciousness at any portion of that still-writhing body. "You stole our laughter and gave us sweat and tears. You took our life of ease and gave us drudgery. You took our innocence and cursed usss with knowledge!"

She was weeping helplessly.

And so was someone else.

Cain. It had to be Cain.

Inhaling raggedly, she strained toward an evenness, which could deal with Cain. With what she had done to him.

She wiped a hand across her eyes, clearing the haze of her passion as well as her tears.

The snake was dead. Splattered. Flattened. Oozing. Eve shivered with self-revulsion. She'd never suspected such potential within herself.

A sharp pain—surely only exertion—shot through her bowels.

Cain huddled far back in shadows. He was sobbing, but his eyes were wide. Frightened.

Pressing her hand low, against renewed pain, she moved one step toward him.

Drawing his breath on a quivering plea, he flattened himself against the boulder that restrained him from further retreat. Slowly, watchfully, he pushed to his feet.

How could she explain what had happened to her? How could she convince him that none of her anger had been for him?

Of course she couldn't. Not then. Even if she were able to speak calmly, he was incapable, just then, of hearing. And the pain! Sparks of it, flying through her.

Let him run to the shelter of the tent, or of the fields, and draw his solace from whatever reservoirs he held within. Certainly, she had alienated herself from him for now.

Perhaps forever.

She turned, huddling over her pain, listening to his relieved breathing, for his scrabbling toward escape.

Long after his running steps were inaudible (he had gone to the field; she wasn't surprised), she turned to the snake again.

Hurrying against untimely labor, she quickly covered the flattened coils—each scale, each smear of blood, smothered with dust. Not that she might spare Cain, should he return that way. Not even that she might do penance for her violence. (She felt, even then, that the loss of her unborn child would be required for that.) But that she might hide as thoroughly as she hid the battered body, perhaps forever, that hatred she still sometimes bore herself.

Part II

Five

Another harvest.

Shaping the celebration cakes swiftly, deftly, and laying them in neat rows on the wooden table, Eve smiled.

It seemed that she could chart the progress of their lives by counting harvests. Just last year, after harvest, Lese and Pharim had said their marriage vows before the sunlit altar. Hand in hand and eagerly, they'd hurried from sight, toward their own lives, their own fields, their own hardships and joys. Already, Lese was nursing twins—fine sons, ruddy and hungry.

The harvest before that, Ayra had borne her fifth.

Her fifth! And already her sixth was seeded.

Eve shook her head.

It seemed that the pace of years quickened, like a wind, gathering speed, first stroking the grass gently, then swelling and maturing until it had the power to bow trees to the ground.

Sometimes snapping them off, she thought. And her mood sobered.

There had been the autumn when Deri, long barren, had died in childbirth. Deri. Always so willing. Needing approval. Her child seemed much more carefree.

There had been the long-ago harvest celebration, when Abel's music had angered Cain.

Not that their quarreling was unusual. From the earliest days of childhood, when Cain had pinned Abel's arms and held him helpless, they'd quarreled. And yet they had also enjoyed times of great sharing.

When Abel was injured in a fall from the granary rafters, Cain had served him tirelessly through his convalescence.

Eve smiled, remembering. She suspected that Abel had milked that opportunity of service to its full potential.

When Abel's flocks were attacked one night by wolves, Cain had rushed half-dressed from the house. Unarmed, he'd stormed at the snarling animals, waving his arms, shrieking threats, pelting them with clods, with stones, with anything at hand.

And when Cain's fields had withered in drought, Abel had rigged a system of leather shoulder-bands, by which more buckets could be carried with less strain.

In crisis, they were helpers—even partners; at all other times, competitors.

Leaving the cakes to rise, Eve dusted her hands down the fabric of her robe and turned to the vegetables, waiting in heaps to be chopped or cut into wedges. The heavy pot was heating over the coals, the savory herbs sending up whisperings of flavor.

At first, Cain had initiated competitions that tested only physical strength. And always Cain had left the conflict with shoulders a bit straighter, and a small, humorless smile. Not yet satisfied. And always Abel would sigh, touch some scraped or tender stretch of skin or muscle, and turn to other things. Apparently undaunted.

Until, Eve remembered, discarding roots and stems and bruises, Abel's muscles had bronzed and bulged from struggling with his herds. With his height finally approaching Cain's, Abel had often won.

After that, Cain had avoided physical tests, but had welcomed intellectual competition.

Listening for the younger children, laid to their naps, Eve dropped the final vegetables into the pot. She moved to the bread, risen in its bowl. While she poked experimentally, testing its readiness, she thought of those many evening mealtimes when Adam computed the amount of seeds required for a certain plot, or guessed the sacks still left in one of the barns—and the two boys would argue heatedly. Then Cain would rush from the house, determined to prove correctness.

If right, he'd come back crowing and smiling through the remainder of the meal, recounting his accuracy until Eve yearned for all of them to be gone.

If he'd been wrong, he'd return quietly, later, after the meal was cleared. He'd kiss Eve's cheek, or even help her, offering to take the scraps to the chickens. He'd never mention the matter again. Nor, to his credit, would Abel.

Shaping the small loaves, she sighed. So much energy they'd wasted, those two. So much time dedicated to disagreement that should have been spent on sharing.

The other boys who'd settled nearby to raise their families—Bern, Rabul, Benij, Zun, and Mattil—showed respect and admiration for both their older brothers; but there were times when divided loyalties split their ranks, as well. Of the girls, only Sael backed Cain. Always a large girl, rough and ungainly, she seemed to worship the stubborn man. Whenever she was needed for household chores, she'd have gone early to the fields with him. And, while he seemed to spurn her friendship in public, even reducing her to tears at times, there was a bond, Eve was sure, that stretched in both directions.

Strange how bonds formed. Not just those among the children here, while they remained—but as they spread and married, forming new alliances, new unions, new intrigues. Sometimes she wondered about those distant groups— Palie and Krim and all their growing brood . . . Sarna and Um, who'd followed them . . . and all those others who, from time to time, fell away like the petals of pear blossoms. Were they all well? All happy? Did they remember, as she did so clearly, the difficult lessons learned in childhood? Did they remember *God?*

Shaping the last of the bread, Eve took the bowl to the dooryard, where she scraped the final flakes for the chickens. Studying her immediate world, she tabulated the changes, which had occurred, year by year.

The tent was gone. Its skins now covered bales of straw. One section stretched across a wooden framework to shelter the spring from fallen leaves and other debris.

The original shelter had long ago been disassembled. Those skins lay, almost forgotten, as barriers beneath loose grain in granary bins, a protection against rising dew.

The house sat closer to the stream. Lush willows shaded it, keeping it cool in summer. (Cooler, at least, than the tent had been.) Adam and the boys had carried clay from the hillside, blended it with mud and sand and small pebbles, reinforced it with wood and stone, and built a sturdy structure. While not spacious, it was roomy enough—their living-quarters extended to the out-of-doors when weather allowed.

Smiling, Eve stroked the wide doorpost.

Her house.

It is good, she thought.

It is good. The words echoed within her, and turned there, comfortably—a warm tie to that early, childlike exuberance in Eden. There, happiness had been assured. Untested, and therefore barely tasted. Unappreciated. They had accepted without thought or thankfulness the ease, the comfort, the lack of concern. God's hand, touching theirs; His voice, a daily nearness.

His voice saying, "It is good." All taken for granted.

How she had yearned, through the years, to hear that voice once more, to feel that tangible presence. Never, if she could hear God's voice again, would she accept it lightly, never cease to praise Him for His love. Of course, she praised Him in any event, and felt an habitual rightness. A voiceless affirmation, which, when it came, urged her to further prayer that once again they might see Him—Adam, she, their children. That His voice might make His presence as real as the textures of stone and leaf and wood and running water.

And . . . her hand stilled on the sun-warm doorpost. She had never spoken of it, even to Adam, since any questioning—especially her own—might shatter the tenuous sensation, which occurred increasingly in response to her prayer. But she was sure (or nearly sure) that there had been something. Not quite a voice, yet. Perhaps later.

Oh, surely later! At first she had thought it a swelling in her ears, that buzzing and humming which sometimes accompanies fever. She had pushed with her fingertips, rubbing gently, wanting it to clear.

That is, until she wondered: Might it instead be God's whispering? God's initial reply to her need for tangible assurance?

Each time, her ears had strained, reached, expanded.

Nothing. The buzzing gone. But if the swelling disappeared without an application of warmed herbs, might that not prove—?

Please, God. Please. If it was *your voice* . . .

Nothing. Not then. And when, weeks later, the sensation had recurred, again at the close of intense and needful prayer, once more her questioning. Her doubt. Not that God could do it, but that He had.

For surely, if He were to speak to anyone, wouldn't it be to Adam? Not that she suffered, still, the initial intensity of her guilt (surely she had earned release through toil, with penance, with prayer, with the coin of grief). But it seemed that Adam, first from God's shaping hands, should be the first to sense a lessening of distance.

And how could Adam not have mentioned such an event to her?

She stirred, wanting—yet not wanting—to resume her preparations for the evening's ceremony. Her spirit required just one more moment of quiet aloneness, reaching toward God.

Please, she prayed, *now, at another harvest, let us know, with certainty . . .*

Again, the reaching cells, straining for sound. Again, the gentle swelling, within. The movement in her mind. *It is good.* A tiny whispering! No more.

She was content. She must be content—for then, at least. The baking fire was hot, the bread ready.

A flurry of sound from the sheep pens caught her attention, and she waited, watching as Adam and Abel strode, side by side, each carrying a perfect lamb across his shoulders.

For the sacrifice, she knew, and shivered slightly.

That a God of life be worshiped through death still struck discord in her heart. And the more she sought to make her spirit sing, as Adam's obviously did, the more discordant were the notes.

Abel's voice, quickened by excitement, carried to her, and Adam's laughter rang out, rich and hearty. The lamb struggled on his shoulders, then quieted.

Eve exulted in the strength of Adam's stride, in his confidence as he called to the other boys, who'd been gathering firewood. All but Cain. Cain would make his own sacrifice this year, he'd said. And—half a beat later—Abel had said that he would, too.

Since a long-past harvest festival, when Abel had shaken a handheld instrument of bronze and copper with tiny metal shapes which sang against one another, music had become increasingly important. Once recovered from his initial jealousy, Cain had fashioned a drum of copper and stretched-taut oxhide. The rubbed-bright metal gleamed in firelight each night as they recited the Creation Hymn. Abel's chiming instrument seemed dull by comparison.

That next harvest, Abel had taken gourds, drying them carefully over winter, the seeds hardening within. He'd painted each instrument with berry juices, and polished the slender curves with sheep-fat. When shaken, the gourds produced crisp, pattering sounds that complemented the clang of metal and pulsing of drums.

And Cain had fashioned a whistle—longer than those Adam still made for the smaller children—and carved it with such delicacy that its melody was clear and sweet and firm, weaving intricate embellishments across the night sounds.

Hearing it, that first time and ever afterward, Eve had hugged her knees, rocking slightly, closing her eyelids against the tears the lovely tones elicited.

And Abel had clasped his brother to his breast. "For me," he ventured huskily, "it brings God closer than He has ever been before."

And so that particular competition between the brothers had closed four harvests after its beginning, when Cain's young beard still struggled toward shape, and Abel had established clearly that, for him, the flocks were more important than the fields.

Shooing the youngest children to a safe distance, Eve removed the perfectly browned loaves of bread from the glowing oven and set them to cool. Eyes serious and small mouth puckered in concentration, Realia carefully greased the crusty tops, while Delya waited with imperfect patience to cover them with linen cloths.

Smiling, Eve arranged the small cakes within the chamber and replaced the stone cover.

Cain had returned moments ago. He threw a small smile of gratitude to Sael, who polished his old drum and guarded it against the younger children, pressing close to thump it. With his recognition, she seemed to expand, plying her polishing cloth with renewed vigor.

Eve's heart ached for both of them—needing approval so desperately, and so often doing exactly what would earn disapproval. Sael's recent refusal to marry at Adam's direction was a case in point. She had stood, slumped yet stolid, an ugly red staining her set features; allowing his words to strike her without denting her determination.

"Frustrating lump!" Adam had sighed once she'd gone. "Does she hope to cling to you like a burdock all her years?"

In her thoughts only, Eve answered, *No. She hopes only to wait at the boundaries of Cain's life.* And she wept inwardly for the ungainly girl—no competition for the light and pretty maidens who fluttered, always, where male eyes might chance to touch.

But she had little time for solemn thoughts, with the celebration so nearly ready.

Feeling like a hen with a triple setting of chicks, Eve herded the youngest girls into a semicircle far from the altar. Adam was allowing the boys to take part, and each wore on his young face a glow that surely belonged in Eden.

Eden.

She smiled ruefully. How long it had been since she'd thought consciously, twice in one day, of Eden! There were occasional mornings when she awoke with the flavor of perfect tranquility still in her mind. When she sensed the perfume of Eden's flowers swirling about her, and—almost—felt the splash of her favorite waterfall.

She shrugged.

Eden lay in the past. Another world. Except for the Creation Hymn, which kept it tangible, it might have sprung from fancy.

Her world was here, where children cried and wiped their runny noses against her neck, where bees stung and thorns ripped and brambles overran and tempers flared, where love ebbed and flowed—sometimes curdling, often blooming.

Deri's child ran to her, hugging her about the thighs. Then Ayra's four appeared, toddling in graduated sizes—her fifth hugging his mother's neck, her sixth already beginning to show in her rounded belly.

The area filled quickly. Noisily. Still, when Adam raised his hands for the beginning of the Creation Hymn, all were attentive. Even the youngest of the children seemed to sense solemnity.

The instruments began. The stanzas rose in flowing cadences.

It is good, thought Eve, tears starting. So good.

And God's whisper, more audible now—agreeing—startled her emotions to deeper warmth.

"Thank you," she murmured.

Following the Hymn, Adam recited once again his litany of thanksgiving for harvest. Then, with casual skill, he killed and offered up his sacrifice—a firstling lamb.

Eve marveled at how he shone with dignity, despite the bloodstains on his robe and arms. At such times, she could sense his Godlikeness, those elements God had kneaded into him when shaping him from dust, and garnished with His own glorious breath. Elements, she had admitted with sadness over and over, through the years, that found only pale imitation in any of their sons. God's promise still waited, somewhere beyond the present.

Adam had scarcely brushed the tinder with flame when fire erupted, roaring, consuming the lamb, licking, devouring with great gulping swallows the sacrifice he had laid. A shout of praise accompanied the billowing smoke toward Heaven.

Adam stepped back from the altar. "Cain?" he offered softly.

"Let . . . let Abel precede me, my father."

Adam's eyebrows raised, and Eve felt a sudden chill.

Adam made a slight gesture of acceptance. "Abel, then."

Abel approached the altar, his expression serious, his movement careful, as though some slight stumbling might be an offense to God. His lamb squirmed in his arms, and he quieted it, gently. It waited at his command as he freed the altar of any slight debris, then arranged fresh tinder on its surface. Eve could see that slight rising film, which betrayed a remainder of heat.

The lamb's shed blood spattered and sizzled, then flowed down the sides of the altar, cooling the rock. Abel motioned, and Lunt came, tugging another lamb, while Marik ceremoniously offered heaps of yellow fat. All in readiness, the younger brothers backed away.

Lifting his arms toward Heaven, Abel raised his voice in ringing praise. Not really taking note of the words, Eve listened instead to the poetic flow of syllables, to the musical quality of his voice, to its rise and fall, its undulations from vibrant praise to hushed humility. She glanced toward Adam. His face shone, both with pride in his son, she felt, and in sympathy with the words of praise.

As Abel lowered his arms and reached to ignite the tinder, flame erupted while his torch remained a cubit or more away. Stronger and fiercer even than Adam's flame, this roared and surged and enveloped—its heat so intense that

Eve didn't need to urge the younger children to move farther back.

And, within its roaring, Eve heard God's voice trumpeting, *"It is good!"*

At last! Eve's heart expanded. Surely, at last, God had broken his long silence!

With a moan, Abel prostrated himself near the foot of the altar.

Eve's heart spoke gratitude. Her lips shaped soundless words of praise. Could it be Abel, then, after all? God had honored the sacrifice of their son, beyond any honor He had shown them since their expulsion from Eden. She had no fear for Abel, lying there so close to the flames; God would protect him.

Surely, this was a day of new promise. A promise of closeness, once more. Of daily dialogue. Of oneness.

Dared she hope for this? Pray for this? Her breathing quickened, and she, too, lifted her arms, her head bowing, her spirit lifting, her mind reaching out to God—not forming words, for there could be no words to express that stretching of her mind and soul toward Him.

How long she stayed thus, she couldn't know. She felt no aching in her back and arms, no tiring of her spirit. But at last something within her said that it was enough, that God knew her yearning, that He had acknowledged her worship.

The flame was gone, the last wisps of smoke drifting upward like the final dying note of a hymn. Abel rose slowly, his face glowing, his eyes glazed.

Still, when Cain moved toward the altar, Abel found his voice. "Could I help you, brother?" he asked. But Cain brushed by him, not answering.

There was determination on Cain's face, Eve noted. And a *need* expressed there, as she had so often read it. This time, no loving words or gentle pat of hers could suffice. He needed *God's* approval.

Please, God, she thought, *accept his lamb, as well.*

She had seen no lamb, she realized suddenly. Only Adam's and Abel's. Looking about, she searched for it, seeing only a skin-draped basket, broad, but shallow. Too shallow, certainly, to contain a living animal.

Methodically, Cain arranged the tinder. Then, while Sael throbbed the muted drum, he intoned his prayer of thanksgiving for the abundance of the earth; the texture of grain, and its flavor; the blessings of dew and of sunlight.

When he had finished, he strode ceremoniously to the large basket, removed its cover, and bore to the altar great armfuls of wheat stalks, heavy with grain . . . of oats, the straw golden and glittering . . . of barley, heavy and ripe and perfect. He carried large, glowing bunches of grapes, and great, perfect fruits, the best of each species. There were fruits of the tuberous plants, washed and polished. "The first fruits of my harvest, Oh God!" he cried.

A harsh wind whispered in the grasses, muttered in the palms, rattled in the drying olive leaves. A dark cloud covered the sun.

Carefully, Cain touched the torch to the tinder.

It sputtered briefly.

Again.

Wind snatched the flame away, nearly extinguishing the torch.

Again.

A few twig ends glowed, then died to darkness.

Again . . . and again . . . and again—

Cain's expression struggled through disappointment and jealousy, frustration, and, at last, achieved rage. He snuffed the torch in the dust, snapped its sticks across his lifted knee, swept from the altar the fruits he had so carefully arranged there.

Oh, my poor, dear Cain, mourned Eve in her heart. She felt Adam's hand on her shoulder in shared sympathy.

"Why are you angry?" asked a voice, with more of sorrow in its tones than of answering anger.

Eve recognized God's voice as she and Adam had heard it in Eden, prior to the expulsion. His voice seemed less wounded now. She heard less evidence of His personal loss. Perhaps, through the years, God had grown accustomed to disappointment.

"And why is your countenance fallen?" the voice continued, filling the world with its quiet insistence. "If you do well, shall you not be accepted? And if you do not well, sin lies at the door." God's voice hushed. Only a wind whispered, then, and a wind chilled Eve's spirit, as well. Why should it be—just when she'd thought the distance melted, just when she'd supposed Eden's rightness restored—that God's most audible words must be of condemnation, however quiet, however sad?

And yet, somewhere within her, a "something" whispered. An element of calmness? Of comfort? Later, when she had time for thought, she might assess it.

For now, there was only Cain.

Cain's discarded sacrifice lay littered about the altar. Everyone remained still, as though action might fracture something fragile, producing something dangerous.

And then Cain moved. His face, when he lifted it, was set in lines of grim purpose. Fists clenched, back stiff, he hurried toward his fields.

His movement seemed to free them all.

"*What* sin?" Sael was sputtering, the drum clutched tightly to her breast. "What sin has Cain committed that Abel hasn't? Why is one sacrifice so . . . so . . ." Breaking into sobs, she ran toward the house.

At least not to Cain, Eve thought. *But I must go to Cain.*

She moved slowly, head down, wondering what she might say. How she dared say anything to take the sting from God's words.

"Eve."

She waited for Adam. "I fear for Cain," she said.

"I, too." He paused to turn her toward him for a moment's tenderness. "But Abel has gone to talk with him. That may help."

Perhaps. None of the others, she knew, had Abel's ability to heal with words. Yet doubt blew like a cold wind across her heart. There'd always been such rivalry—

Still, God was with them. He favored Abel, that much was obvious, and would protect him. And Abel would want only to soothe and comfort Cain.

Numbly, she packed Cain's knapsack. With hard, round cheeses. With dried mutton, in long chewy strands which would stave off hunger for hours. With wedges of dried fruit, and loaves of unleavened bread, small—to conserve space.

Bulging waterskins hung from thongs, shoulder to opposite armpit, sloshing when he walked.

"Where will you go, my son?" she asked, her voice like a dead reed.

"Somewhere"—he cleared his throat—"east of Eden."

"East of Eden," she repeated dully. "That could be so far—"

"It will be," he agreed. "It must be."

She lifted her glance to his face and watched it contort with grief.

"Never again to till the soil and see it bloom beneath my fingers—"

She reached, and he came to her, allowing her to comfort him. *God has a way of punishing,* she thought, *by taking that which is best-loved.*

Like Abel. Each hour, the loss of Abel was like a chasm in her heart.

Yet it hadn't been God who took Abel. Still, she thought rigidly, it had been God who allowed it to happen. *As He had allowed them to sin in Eden.* The thought came swiftly. Unbidden. Like an echo of her earlier questionings. God had permitted their weakness in the face of temptation. Had, indeed, permitted the temptation. Had He—and the natural progression of her questioning both shocked and frightened her—had He *wanted* them to sin?

No! her thoughts shrieked, and she pushed herself from Cain, turning from him.

"No," a softer certainty sighed within her.

She held herself still, listening inwardly.

"I needed you here," the sigh continued. "I am lonely."

She closed her eyes against tears of gratitude. God missed them, as they so often yearned for Him.

So caught had she been in the tangle of her doubting, in the warmth of His unexpected assurance, that she failed to consider how Cain must interpret her actions.

His voice was shattered as he asked, "Can you ever forgive me, Mother?"

The moment she'd found him, wretched and stunned, cradling Abel's bloody corpse, she had forgiven him.

And new knowledge stirred within her soul. In just that way, had God forgiven them—because He loved them? The punishment must still be carried out, both theirs and Cain's. Yet the love remained.

"We will always love you, my son," she reassured him.

He straightened. He'd changed greatly these past terrible days. She saw lines of new character etched on his face. And lines of sorrow. Of calmness. Of maturity. The mark God had written on his forehead sometimes seemed scarcely noticeable.

Perhaps, Eve thought, it shows more clearly when it's needed, to broadcast God's protection.

Cain touched it. "In a way," he said quietly, "I wish He hadn't put it there. I was so afraid, at first, that men might kill me. Now, there are moments when I wish . . ."

She stopped him with her fingers to his lips. "No. To lose one son is—" She shook her head, unable to frame words that expressed her inability to endure the loss of another.

And yet she *was* losing him. Though perhaps not quite forever.

"You lost the wrong son, Mother."

"*No!*" And, again, she couldn't phrase the thought that there was no right one to lose. "You . . . will be careful."

"Yes." He touched his forehead again, as though the mark were a talisman.

"You will remember, each night, to repeat the Creation Hymn."

That time, an answer came less readily.

"It must be remembered," she said firmly.

He hugged her once—quickly, roughly—and then he was off.

She didn't—she couldn't—walk to the doorway to watch him out of sight. She didn't know, and never asked, if Adam walked with him a way. Or even said farewell.

And it wasn't until much later that day that she realized that Sael was gone, too.

That first week, with Abel and Cain both gone, Adam refused even to attempt their evening ritual. Without their voices joining, without their music, Eve felt that she couldn't have borne it anyway.

The second week, having fallen out of the habit, the ritual was easier to avoid.

But one late afternoon she sought Adam, meaning to urge him to reinstate the practice, and found him sitting in shadows, tossing pebbles to the stream. Beside him lay a wineskin, nearly flat. And she grumbled within, cursing the discovery he and Cain had made together. That alchemy of long-neglected fruit or grain, fermenting into wine.

She herself hated the taste of it, and Abel had always spurned it. But Cain had drunk of it often, after a long, hot day of work, and pronounced it refreshing. And Adam, occasionally, had enjoyed it, too.

Gently, she took away the skin and left him brooding.

That evening, they resumed the ritual. Much of its fire was gone, and Adam stumbled often. But she and the children kept the phrases flowing well enough.

And once again, with an unexpected warming, she felt a momentary stirring of assurance. God was pleased. Surely, that was it.

In the silence that followed the final lines, she went to Adam, touching his arm, urging him to return with her to bed. But he thrust her hand away. So she left without him, with the children, trying to make their bedtime ordinary. They'd known sadness enough since Abel's death and Cain's and Sael's departure; she wouldn't add to it with her own.

But there was no sleep for her.

When she closed her eyes, images of Cain's anger and Abel's bloodstained body rose before her. With her eyes open, she read the changing shadows on the wall and thought of Adam. What would become of them? Of their love? Would he ever regain his stature? His stride? His pride in his work? His enthusiastic praise to God?

Shadows shifted on the wall, marking the passing hours. She rose and moved about the house, but her rustlings broke the children's sleep.

Where was he?

What was he doing? If she had thought he talked with God, she'd have gone to sleep, at ease. But she knew a feeling of unrest. Of disquietude.

At last, she slipped into her sandals and went to find him.

Sheep stirred in their pens.

Not there.

Not in the goat-sheds, either.

The oxen milled heavily in the pasture field, grazing.

Not there.

Nor by the stream, which murmured sleepily above its bed of rocks.

She scanned the open fields, searching for a shadow, which might approximate his shape.

Not there.

By the altar? Fearfully, she walked that way. The altar loomed dark against the night sky.

Not there, either.

She stared beyond, toward the farther fields, moving with wind and life. If he were there . . .

She feared that lions lurked there, hungry for any blood. But Adam knew the dangers, too. Surely he wouldn't go there.

The granaries. She hadn't searched the granaries.

She found him there, drunkenly asleep, another wineskin oozing a few ill-smelling drops beside him.

"Adam." She spoke softly, shaking him gently. Rats scurried in the shadows, slipping on grain. She shivered. "Adam."

He grumbled, stirring, pushing her hand away.

"Adam, please don't grieve this way."

He turned heavily, muttering.

"Adam—"

His snore rattled.

In the end, she lay beside him, the grain a shifting pallet, but not unpleasant. She had meant to lie there only moments, hoping that he'd rouse and go with her. She wouldn't leave the children alone for long . . .

She woke suddenly. The shafts of moonlight had shifted again.

"Adam?" she gasped, starting up, but he was on her—heavy, fierce, his hands harsh and demanding.

Later, she lay still and chastened. Never had he taken her in that way before. Never had he struck her. Never had he cursed her, calling her carrion, saying that she alone had robbed him of all he loved. That she had brought him sin and cost him God and Eden. And that now she had cost him his oldest sons.

He came to himself while they lay together, spent and sweating. She was aware of the moment when he became—almost—himself again. Though could she ever again be sure just who and what the true Adam was?

"Eve," he began. "What . . . why are we here?" His words were only slightly slurred.

She couldn't answer.

"We—" Suddenly, he seemed fully awake. Frightened. "*What's happened here?*"

Despite herself, she was weeping softly.

"Dear God, what—" His hands groped, and she stiffened against them. He drew back. She sensed his confusion. *He doesn't know,* she thought. He couldn't have known. It was the wine. The cursed wine.

"The wine," he whispered dully. "The wine . . . and oh, dear Eve—I've hurt you, haven't I?"

He could never know in how many ways.

"And . . ." He pulled himself fully away and finished, agony in his tones, "I've . . . shamed you."

If God would hear her, if she were worth the hearing, she prayed with her soul that no child would result from this night.

She sighed quiveringly. It was the wine that had bruised her. The wine that had whispered obscene denials of their unity. The man, Adam, she still loved and needed.

And that man was suffering. And yet, to ease his anguish must compound her own.

She forced herself toward control. "It is nothing," she murmured at last. And, straightening her clothing, she moved toward the edge of the grain bin.

Pain shot through her cheekbone, through her shoulder, through her thigh, and she stifled a whimper.

"Nothing," he ridiculed softly, tears in his voice.

Her eyes stung. Nothing, at least, that she could deal with at that moment.

"As you said, Adam, the wine—"

He groped for the skin and flung it violently across the width of the granary. Rats squealed their fright. The scrambling of small feet on shifting grain continued while she pulled herself from the bin, found her sandals, and moved stiffly toward the door. Adam followed almost silently, having made no further attempt to touch her since her rebuff.

On their pallet, she held herself tightly away.

He wept quietly while she lay, sorting her thoughts and choosing those to be discarded forever—if it were possible—from those which one day, when she felt more capable, she must share with him.

When he was quieter, he promised her, "I'll not touch wine again."

For the moment, it was enough. The wine had been his undoing, as the serpent had been hers.

She touched his tear-wet cheek, and fell asleep.

Eve's visible bruises healed, but each time Adam looked at her, he winced.

"Please," he begged of her, more than once. "Please tell me what happened." He needed to know, he explained, so that he could ask her forgiveness more specifically. Hers and God's.

And she tried.

She tried as she worked at her tangled yarn, while he carved a new stopper for an urn. But her voice deteriorated. Strangled in tears. Dropping his head in his hands, he wept great, wracking sobs she knew she lacked the power to quell, as long as her trembling fingers stopped short of touching his shoulder.

She tried as they waded thigh-deep in the stream, repairing a break in the dam. The sun, high and dazzling, casting a brilliance to narrow her eyes and burn through her robe to her shoulders, lost its heat as he asked still again. Fumbling, she dropped a stone, feeling its wash as it fell, and ignoring the sharp stab of pain as it grazed past her ankle. When her mind shrank from memories like wounds still seeping, what could a stone-bruise matter?

Whenever she had worked until she stumbled toward their pallet, eyes already half-closed, breathing already sleep-heavy, and he asked her—yet again—she tried. But to grope through her thoughts was like moving through clotted cream. Her mind wouldn't focus. Numbly, she knew that her answer, when it came, must be carefully shaped and delivered.

For she recognized, as time went on, that her answer must soon be given. She found safety in avoidance, but she could read the price in Adam's expression. The lines of his mouth, once tending upward, had settled into anguish. His eyes, once brightening whenever their glances met, now glazed with pain.

But how could she shape phrases that would heal, rather than deepen, Adam's wounds? How could she, for her own sake, resurrect those painful moments in all their harsh detail? How could she tell him the truth without becoming his judge? Or, worse yet, his martyr?

God help me, she prayed. *Give me the words. Give me the opportunity.*

And yet, when it came, she nearly missed the moment.

They were pruning vines, and Adam's knife had slipped, cutting too deeply. His shoulders sagged.

"But remember," she urged, gently taking the branch. "Last year . . . and only see—" She gestured toward a healthy tree, taller and fuller than others its age. Adam had thought the tree damaged beyond repair. And, from his guilt, he had lavished it with care.

It is time.

The stirring was within her. The rightness. Straightening, drawing deeply of the cool air, she reached for Adam's hand. "The tree forgave you," she said, not even considering how foolish that might sound. "As I have long since forgiven you."

She heard his harsh intake of breath, and tried to still her own quickened heartbeat. Never had she loved him more. Never had it been so vital that she express her caring.

Leading him to a shadowed spot by the stream, she added, "You know that God forgives. Now, my love, it is essential that you forgive yourself."

He asked with childlike eagerness, "You'll tell me . . . everything?"

"Everything," she promised, and knew that, should she falter, God Himself would supply the healing words.

Six

She had thought never to be happy again. But she was happy.

She had thought never to have laughed lightheartedly again. But she was laughing. Even giggling, as Adam stood before her, sweaty and dung-stained and almost hidden behind a giant bouquet of flowers.

"It was the only way," he said, "that I could offer you a sweet and pleasing fragrance. Mine is more pungent."

His "pungent" odor was apparent even over the mingled scents of the flowers. And so she told him as he caught her close, pasting their bodies together with his sweat, he sharing her smudges of flour and berry juice, she sharing his sheep-pen stains.

It had been good, she thought, this healing time. This learning to forgive at greater depth. This learning to know one another in a different way.

These past ten months had been sweet in a way she had never known before she'd felt his violence. It was as though he had reawakened motherhood in her, and it had turned toward him, protectively, rather than to their babes.

And she was with child again. She'd known it even before the monthly sign proclaimed it. She was with child!

Her whole being sang praise to God. Not that this child could take Abel's place. Nor Cain's, for that matter. He would be a person of his own, filling a special chamber of her heart, as memory of each of them resided there. But knowing that he was there, growing within her, healed many scars. And holding him in her arms would heal many, many more.

And he'd soothe Adam's remaining scars, as well.

During the winter months, while the earth lay fallow, she and the daughters still at home spun and wove. There was something comforting about the texture of new yarn, something which encouraged remembering and dreaming. Sometimes they'd work quietly, but often the girls would ask what it had been like before they were born, what it had been like in Eden, what life might be like when they were her age.

What *would* it be like? she wondered.

Already, many farms nestled in distant valleys, while a town grew near the center of this crowded plain. Benij had said that some of the townsmen were digging a common well, that already the first stones had been laid in place.

Not to have our own water, Eve thought, shaking her head. She wouldn't like that. To depend on their spring and the streams for their needs . . . to have a quiet place, where her thoughts could flow as clearly as cool water filling her waterskin or jug. Surely, that was the way it was meant to be. At a common well—she shuddered, imagining the gossip, the quarrels, the hurt feelings, the wasted hours.

Adam expressed his displeasure in another way. "Where several women are gathered together," he said, half-joking, half-grim, "several husbands are being discussed and compared."

Inwardly, Eve agreed. Already, she'd chided some of her daughters and granddaughters for just such idle chatter.

"Of course," Adam added, grinning, "where several men are gathered together . . ."

"You don't!" she said, feigning anger.

"I was thinking of the younger, more courageous men!"

Ah, how she loved those twinkling eyes! The way his mouth lifted at the corners when he teased. The way his muscles rippled beneath the smooth cloth garment she had woven him.

She felt her expression turn soft, and saw him notice. Swiftly, he moved toward her, catching her in his arms, pressing her close—as close as the growing child would allow—kissing the tip of her nose, her eyelids, while her knees weakened, and his arms tightened and lifted. "The younger men," he repeated softly, "have less reason than I for contentment and pride."

She caught their younger daughters watching, nudging one another. May they one day know such love, she thought. May God grant them such contentment and joy.

The child leapt in her womb, and she patted against it. Adam smiled down, but kept his arms folded across his chest, where he'd placed them when the girls showed such obvious interest. As though our loving were unnatural, Eve thought, but tenderly. As though we were too old for tenderness, for passion.

Never too old, she thought, and touched Adam's arm in passing on her way to the storeroom for more flax.

Just as this pregnancy had lacked complications, so her labor was short and easy.

"You have borne another fine son for my father," Ayra said proudly.

For many years, now, Ayra had served as midwife—not only for Eve, but for many of the other women. Her brisk gentleness comforted, while inviting perfect confidence. There was about her no nonsense, no hesitancy as she slapped a babe to its crying breath and cleansed it, the mother, and the birthing area.

Cradling her newest son, crooning to him, Eve remembered Cain's birth, and Abel's, and Deri's, and Palie's, and at least a dozen of the others—Ayra's own, in fact—when Adam had tended her. For those first few births his anguish had added to her own, yet warmed her, proving that she was cherished and needed.

Now, like other husbands, he was banished from hearing distance.

"These men," Ayra said with a sniff. "It shames them if their women cry out. But let a hammer strike their thumbs, and they take to their pallets in pain."

Eve laughed softly. Not Adam, she thought. Adam had encouraged her to cry, and had himself cried.

But she would not say that to Ayra, whose home life was less gentle.

"Dear Ayra," she said, wanting to make up for that lack, "you've done well, as always."

"And you, my mother."

Eve smiled over Seth's head. She and Adam had agreed that Seth would be his name, but she wouldn't speak it until he'd "decided" more publicly. "You have such a talent, Ayra, both with the babes and with their mothers."

Ayra's briskness softened. She dropped to her knees, catching Eve's free hand in hers. "You taught me gentleness, my mother. You taught me many skills."

Eve nodded. "But God has taught you more. His love powers your hands, as you do what many women couldn't—"

"—and what *no man* could do!" Ayra finished.

There was a moment's throbbing silence. Then Eve asked, "Have you thanked Him for this gift of yours, my daughter?"

Ayra's glance dropped. Her hands caught together, twisting. Gone was the aura of perfect confidence.

If only, Eve thought, *if only we could bear their problems for them. If only we could spare them pain.*

"Ayra," Eve began.

Slowly, Ayra raised her eyes. They were filled with tears. One fat one plopped to Eve's hand, and they both laughed softly, while Ayra mopped busily at the rest. Seth nuzzled at Eve's swelling breast.

"He's hungry! Already he's hungry!"

"Ayra—"

She had stood, had turned away, busying herself with work already finished. "Now, we must tell my father that he has yet another son!"

When the day came that Adam should pronounce the name in public, Ayra stood close, waiting for Eve to tell her how she still might serve. Her left hand absently patted at her youngest, heavily asleep, his thumb barely touching his slack lower lip.

Many of the others had come. Mattil, who always looked ill, his shoulders hunched, his breathing shallow, an expression of discomfort and distaste in the curve of his colorless lips. Bern, boasting to his brothers of the rich fields he had claimed in a nearby valley. Benij, unaccustomedly quiet—missing Cain? Eve wondered. Zun, burly, dark, his black eyes squinting with what seemed to be perpetual merriment, scarcely suppressed even in the most solemn of moments.

And no wonder, thought Eve, glancing at his squat, rounded wife and numerous plump children. They were like playful puppies—bounding, yipping, scuffling in laughing tangles while their mother frowned, approved, separated, pointed, without ever breaking her flow of animated monologue.

"And the well!" she had sighed, rolling her eyes skyward, her hands describing the movement of flight, enclosing Eve, Ayra, and all the other women clustered nearby. "You wouldn't believe the well! You must come to the city, to see us, and let me take you there! The water—so *much!* More than enough for everyone! And so cool and sweet!" Her eyes half-closed in bliss, she kissed her fingertips resoundingly, yet allowed no break in the bubbling of words. "But best of all, the companionship. No longer must we women labor in isolation, with only the lizards to talk to, or the children, still drugged with sleep. We meet there! And oh, the conversation! So stimulating! I have learned more by the well in an afternoon than I could learn in years from waiting for Zun to inform me!"

He had heard his name, and had turned his merry eyes toward the sound. His expression softened still further. It seemed to Eve that laughter trembled at the corners of his lips.

Some of them are happy, she thought contentedly, then glanced at Ayra, and sighed.

But this was no day for sadness!

There was food to be served—cakes, sweet with the honey that nearly oozed from their pores; fruits, fresh from vine and branch and washed in their own cool spring; bread, soft and mellow, crusted with brown crispness, to be eaten with ripened cheese, or dipped either in the fresh milk of goats or an amber drink, which echoed the flavors of honey and fruit.

And when all had eaten, when only the crumbs remained, when even Zun's small brood, with puffed-out cheeks, proclaimed themselves full and belched to prove it, then there was music so lilting, so impetuous, that it discouraged after-meal napping and coaxed even Ayra's dour husband to dancing.

Crumbs cleared away and thrown to the chickens, Eve settled to watch, Seth nuzzling at her breast. It was good to be together. To celebrate. To bask in God's blessing of new life. To find joy in one another. To be surprised by newly discovered samenesses and diversities.

Her toe tapped to the music. Melody moved through her mind. When she closed her eyes, feeling the sun's warmth on her upraised face, she could imagine the lighter notes to be petals caught in a breeze, or the sparkling of water, sprayed through sunlight.

She must have slept. Her arms were empty—Seth removed, no doubt by Ayra, for his safety. Eve felt a twinge of pique. Just because Ayra assisted at birth, she needn't consider herself a second mother.

But no, Adam held the child. And it was Adam who had startled her awake, though gently.

Her face warmed.

"It's time," he murmured.

Time.

Of course. The music had stopped. Everyone was waiting. And she had slept. She framed an apology, but Adam's smile absolved her. You have given me another son, it seemed to say. You have a right to be tired.

While everyone watched expectantly, Adam pronounced the name, and Eve agreed, saying, "God has appointed me another seed instead of Abel, whom Cain slew."

How difficult it was to say that, even then. To admit that Cain was gone, banished by God, and that he'd lifted up his hand against his brother, killing him as though he were a lamb for sacrifice.

No. Not even that. A sacrificial lamb was chosen carefully and carefully prepared. It was laid softly across the altar, its blood spilled as an act of worship.

Abel's death had been thoughtless. Brutal. An offering only to jealousy and anger.

"But you, Seth," Eve said softly. "You will help us to forget forever."

But he couldn't.

Not when he looked at her with those eyes . . . Cain's eyes, innocent, as they'd once been, . . . and Abel's sweetness.

"This is a special son, I think," said Adam.

"They've all been special. Our daughters, too."

"But this one, this one . . ."

Perhaps, she thought. *Perhaps.* She shrugged hope away. God had given him to them at a special time, that was all, a time of need, of anguish. No, at a time when healing was already in progress after the most grievous wounding of all. Adam's denial of her.

Another harvest, and another, and another. Life paced rather placidly along, segmented by the seasons, by the work that each required.

Seth was succeeded by two sisters, Elena and Kae, and by a brother, Ruel. And still another small one grew within Eve's womb. With each birth, Adam sacrificed a kid or a lamb in thanksgiving. With each, contentment grew.

It was as though they moved in cycles, like the seasons, Eve thought, a cycle of peace, a cycle of pain.

With each pain, though, came growth.

Strange.

She could see that so clearly, looking back. With the greatest anguish had come the greatest growth, just as a child was delivered only through the fiercest travail.

And it wasn't only punishment for sin, was it? Surely God wasn't so cruel. He wasn't cruel at all, she thought, watching the children play.

How beautiful they are. So sweet. And sound.

"So full of promise," God's voice joined her thoughts.

For an instant she remembered that the promise of others, since scattered, had somehow soured as they aged. Not alone with Cain. With so many.

"With some," God admitted.

She shook her head. More *many* than *some*. Men drinking the seasons away, while produce withered in the fields and women, heavy with new children, struggled to feed the ones already born. Some women spending their days in vicious gossip by the village well, as she'd foreseen. Some youngsters, so far removed in generations that Eve could seldom place them in her mind, flirting and flaunting themselves, or framing crude jests behind their jewelled hands.

"And yet," God urged, "there are so many others—who tend their crops and children, who love their families, who purify their thoughts through prayer."

Dismissing His argument, she thought how often, watching the dissipation of promise, she had been moved to anger, wanting to *tell* them—

"But telling," God was smiling, she knew, "telling doesn't always work."

She felt herself flushing. He was thinking of Eden. Of the forbidden fruit. And He was right, of course. Perhaps these descendants of theirs merely needed to learn through pain.

"As you have learned, dear Eve?"

Thoughtfully, she nodded, remembering Ayra—who'd recently lost a child at birth and nearly died herself. Since that loss and near-loss, her husband had softened. And now when Ayra delivered a new babe she spoke only of the father's joy.

If they'd remained in Eden would there have been growth, perhaps, of a different kind? Or would they have been forever children?

For they had been children! She smiled, remembering their hand-in-hand frolics through the Garden. Snatching a fruit and eating it with juice dribbling down their chins. Gathering flowers, which they shared and traded. Talking with God, and never realizing what a marvel that privilege was.

"Mother?"

It was Seth, tugging at her skirt. He stood nearly to her waist, now. Such a bright child, gentle in spirit, but strong enough to be a fine help to his father in the fields and pens.

"Listen to me, Mother!" His eyes snapped with excitement. A bit awkwardly, watching to be sure that he had her full attention, he found a spot in sunlight and used it as a stage. He straightened his shoulders, pressed his hands together, and cleared his throat.

" 'In the beginning, God created the heaven and the earth. And the earth was without form and void.' " He smiled as she gave him her deeper attention. Her hands folded tightly, and on her face played mingled emotions of surprise and pride and gratitude to God. Could it truly be Seth . . . but she closed her mind against the hope that had, far too often, curdled in her breast.

And yet, later, as she gathered Seth close in wordless joy, God's voice vibrated in her ears and through the sunlight, his promise restated.

"He recited the whole thing," she told Adam later, as he washed for the evening meal. "The *whole thing*—never faltering!"

"I wish I'd heard," Adam said wistfully. But Eve rushed ahead.

"Such expression, Adam! Such feeling!" She'd always been thrilled by the Hymn, by its cadences. By the beauty of its phrases. By its power. But it could never have been more powerful, booming in anyone's deeper tones, or shouted by hundreds in chorus, than it had been that day, recited in that young, clear voice, vibrant with belief. All that, she tried to convey, but knew that she'd fallen short.

"Tonight," she promised softly, touching his arm. "Tonight, he could do it for all of us."

Adam reached for the basin, for the wheat-colored towel. "When he's ready," he said.

As she made the final preparations for the meal, she heard him whistling.

The harvest gathered, the sacrifices made, there was a flurry of wedding celebrations.

Once more, the children within traveling distance gathered with those descendants who hadn't broken the ties of family either by choice or by neglect. Once more, the flocks were searched for perfect lambs; fruits were gathered and washed; a space was cleared for dancing; the stones of the oven were heated. Within the house, voices planned, offered, suggested; knives sliced and grated; the flavors of mingled spices anointed the air; and dough met tabletop with resounding thumps and small explosions of flour.

And then, as always, celebration gave way to solemnity and praise.

It always warmed Eve's heart to hear repeated the words Adam had said to her in the early moments of her existence as a woman. "This is now bone of my bones, and flesh of my flesh. . . ." *Blood of my blood,* she would continue in her thoughts. And the unity of spirit—that, above all else. "For this a man shall leave his father and his mother . . ."

These words, meaningless in Eden, had vibrant meaning, now. How many children had she seen joined, only to watch them move blithely out of sight, across the mounded slopes, to other valleys, other plains, where they would till the ground and care for their flocks. Where they would live and quarrel and raise their young. As separate from her as . . . Cain.

Such a short time we have them, she thought.

Even many of those who had settled nearby might as well have been beyond those distant mountains. There were children in the town whom Eve had never met. Even seen with their parents, she couldn't be certain which thread they followed from her and Adam. Yet she might catch a feature, an expression on a tone of voice, which made that connection fleetingly clear.

So many of them. Hundreds, at least, milling through the streets, some having ridden long distances to buy or trade. In the town there were women, whose men were dead or drunken, who spun and wove in trade for produce. There was one young man, crippled and so unable to guide a plow or shear the sheep, who fashioned pottery rich with design—again for trade.

Adam, shaking his head at that, brought clay from the hillside to make their own pots. Where once it hadn't mattered that they leaned a bit to one side, or that the thickness varied, now he examined each carefully, from every angle, and scrawled a decoration with a stick, or added a bit of berry stain for color.

"When we must trade our wool or wheat for someone else's work," he'd say, then shake his head again.

Still, she was glad that the young man had a talent that kept him fed and clothed; and that women, shamed though they must often be, needn't beg for food or see their children hungry. And if she was glad for that, then she must also be happy that there were men less independent than Adam—men willing to buy such services.

Meshanath, they named the new son. His cry was lustier than any she remembered.

His birth was difficult, and Eve noted concern in Ayra's eyes, though she'd kept up a patter of lighthearted talk throughout the hours of labor.

Once he'd been delivered, Ayra's eyes still wore that look, and Eve, holding him limply, knew a weariness, which dragged her into periodic blackness.

How many more children, she wondered, *will it take before the world is sufficiently filled?* Through her blurred mind, the children marched, one after another . . . and their children, and their children's children . . .

Blackness swirled again, claiming her. Dimly, she felt a weight removed. The child. Ayra had taken the child—for its safety?

Eve tried to speak her traditional compliment, but the words seemed twisted, like strands of wool for spinning. Distorted, like shouts down the well in town.

Someone held her hand. "Yes, my mother, you, too have done well. Now, sleep."

The next few days passed in cycles of sleeping, of half-waking, of wearily accepting nourishment, of knowing without seeing him that Adam was there, of feeling the baby nurse, but not holding him.

And then, gradually, she was sitting up. And talking. Trying to hold some sewing, but feeling it drop from her hands while weariness tugged her downward again.

It was weeks, by her count, before she was able to walk without assistance. Another month before she could do her full day's work.

And still another before she felt life surging through her, and heard herself, one day, singing as she kneaded bread.

Aware of a sound in the doorway, she looked up. "Adam! How long have you been standing there?"

"Just long enough—" he began, then shook his head, tears streaming past a twisted smile.

"Oh, Adam . . ."

He accepted her into his arms and clamped her there. He didn't comment on her thinness. He didn't say that he'd been afraid he'd lose her. He didn't need to. And she couldn't tell him how very close she'd felt she was to death.

They stood for a long time there, together, the sleepy sounds of late afternoon milling about them.

At last, she said, "The bread—"

And he, at the same moment, was beginning, "I'll need to call the sheep—"

They laughed together. And the sound was good.

Meshanath grew to be a sturdy, smiling child who followed Seth as closely, Seth often joked, "as a burr to a sheep's fleece." But Seth didn't seem to mind.

Seth had Abel's talent, Eve often thought, of meeting the emotional needs of others. Almost a young man, he showed gentleness with the other children. A willingness to play with them. Yet, with adults, he was an alert and avid listener.

Especially, she'd noticed, when the talk was of God.

"A special son," Adam had said, and he'd been right. This son, sent by God at their time of deepest need, bearing Adam's appearance with the exception of his mother's eyes. This son had seemed to come more directly from God than had any of the others since those early years.

Yet still Eve shrank from hope (perhaps too fervent) that Seth would fulfill God's promise.

"Tell me about God," he'd often urged when, as a child, he'd sat by her feet while the spindle whirred and the wool grew to yarn. "Tell me what it was like to walk with Him."

She noted the difference. The girls, when they asked about Eden, coveted details of the ease of life, or the beauty of birds and flowers. The other boys, those interested in the fields, asked about the various plants which grew there, and how they differed from the ones they knew; those involved with flocks liked best to hear about animals living in peace with one another, predators eating grass. They would sit relaxed, eyes half-closed, and smile or shake their heads. There were times, with some of the children, when Eve was convinced that they thought she spun some fanciful tale to amuse them. There were times, with the sleepy sounds of summer, the lazy buzz of an insect, seeking her shoulder as a resting place, when her words held an air of unreality, even for her. "But it *was* that way," she'd insist, knowing how important it was that their history be perpetuated. "It was only because of the serpent that it ever changed."

With Seth, the comment wasn't necessary. He never questioned her accuracy, but only delved for more details.

"Where, exactly, did you hide? How do you think the eagle knew? Do you suppose she was expelled from Eden, too? I mean because—now that she knew the difference—mightn't she be a problem there? Do you think God's ever sorry He sent you away? Is the angel still *there,* do you think? And does the sword ever burn shorter?"

Such questions forced her backward through time. Forced her to touch areas of thought which had once been too tender for probing. And they excited new direction in her own wondering. But, primarily, they reinforced her growing certainty that here was a special son—special not only to her and to Adam, but special to God.

Surely, God had some great destiny in mind for Seth.

It was good, she thought, watching as Meshanath toddled after him, reaching for a handhold to steady him, that his influence would shape Meshanath's attitudes. Elena, Kae, and Ruel, as well, often observed and imitated him.

"Ruel, especially, can't help but profit," Adam said as he and Eve strolled one Seventh Day afternoon. "There's a wayward strain there—"

His voice broke off, and he paused to hold a whip of blackberry briar from her path, but she knew that he thought of Cain.

Cain.

Often, she wondered where he was. How large his family had grown. Had he followed her admonition to repeat the Creation Hymn each evening, so that his children's children's children would always know how things had come to be? Had he been greatly endangered because of his crime? Had God's mark protected him? Had God's curse afflicted only him, or was it coursing through bloodlines to damn his children, too?

Adam was talking, telling some tale of Ruel and his duties in the sheep pens. She swung her attention to him.

". . . small ribs showing through the fleece," he was saying. "How long his mother had denied him—or why—I couldn't know, but *she* wasn't to blame. She's a dumb animal, after all, not knowing good and evil."

Not knowing good and evil, Eve echoed silently.

". . . but I talked with him all the time we cleaned the stalls, trying to show him his responsibility. Then Seth came along. Not half an hour later, Ruel was whistling and happy, holding that lamb on his lap and nursing it with a cloth nipple bulging with sweetened water—as though *he* were its true mother." He laughed shortly. "I told him, and he resisted, saying it was woman's work, if not the ewe's. Seth talks to him, and he's content." He looked at her, pulling her into his gentle, rueful laughter.

It was a tender afternoon. Resting on that boundary which borders spring and summer, they paused to smell flowers blooming at the stream's brink, and those clustered in shadows, deep in wooded areas. Violets, gentle and fragile, pushed sturdy stems from moss, their marked leaves heart-shaped. Lady slippers bulged their orchid-like blooms, small banners waving.

In the orchards, some trees were blooming, while others already bore infant fruits. Quince, apples, peaches, pears, plums, apricots—

Eve studied them, all together. All acceptable eating, now; while in the Garden, one had been forbidden.

Just as she'd thought the tree unimpressive there, until the serpent tested her, so here, all were equally dusty. Equally heavy in foliage. Equally productive. Their fruits equally delicious and nourishing and lacking in any special qualities of wisdom.

"Do you think we should?" Adam was asking, and she scrambled back from her thoughts.

"I'm sorry, Adam." She laughed lightly. "My thoughts are like tangled yarn today."

"They always are," he teased. "You're always away from me somewhere, even when I have your arm. I can't corral your mind. That's why I never say anything too important."

They laughed together.

"I promise," she said. "I'll cherish every word you say the rest of the afternoon."

Glancing at the declining sun, he laughed again.

"Already!" she said, surprised. "Meshanath will be starved!"

"Meshanath is always starved." He held her to a slow walk.

She didn't struggle. Their shared time was too precious to be rushed. They walked companionably, in silence.

Just as the season trembled on the edge of summer, so day slid toward evening, the sounds and stirrings mirroring that change.

She listened to the murmurings of nesting birds, merging with dying wind and distant water and the wakening rustles of nighttime creatures. Less vivid than daytime sounds. Relaxed . . . and somehow comforting.

A crystal flurry of notes reached her on a breeze, then swept away. Stopping Adam with a hand on his arm, she strained her ears.

Again. It came again.

She glanced at Adam.

"Cain's whistle—?" he whispered, frowning.

She nodded, then shook her head. This was more beautiful, even, than that. "Yet—not a bird."

"No, not a bird."

A moment longer they stood, then moved toward the music. Even after it had faded, they kept the direction.

And soon there was new sound. Delicate. Metallic.

Without doubt, Abel's instrument. The first one. Kept, after his death, in a cloth-lined box. Removed only for shining, for recurrence of memories—

They hurried.

Then slowed again. Joining the mingled flow of notes and jingling metal were voices—now chorused, now parting in harmony.

Eve breathed carefully, deeply. "Beautiful," she whispered on that breath. But Adam shushed her, gently.

She moved cautiously, wanting no rustle of grass or swish of limb or turning of stone to rob them of a single syllable.

When the words became intelligible, they were familiar.

" 'And God called the light Day . . . and the darkness he called Night . . . and the evening and the morning were the first day. . . .' "

Eve blinked back tears.

They found the children in a clearing, sitting on stones that had been gathered, apparently, into a close semicircle. Banked on three sides, sycamores and cedars held the shadows behind them. Vines hung heavily, draped.

Ruel played the whistle—not Cain's after all, but a new one, longer and more delicately carved, even, than his had been. The notes produced fluid music—flowing, breathing, soaring.

Meshanath clutched the handle of the metal instrument Abel had fashioned. Newly shined, it glowed with subdued brilliance in the near-dusk.

Kae and Elena, their faces sweet with concentration, sang a high melody in unison. And Seth's firm tones—usually lower, but sometimes overlapping theirs, and occasionally rising above—wove the harmony.

Pressing Adam's hand, and breathing still with that almost painful control, Eve inhaled the beauty she was hearing, and stored it for later cherishing.

Without moving, they listened until the end.

Only then did the children notice them.

"Ahhhh!" exclaimed Seth, his eyes lighting. "You heard. We were praising our great and precious God."

And throughout the clearing, God's voice reverberated with approval. Even the children heard and sank to their knees in worship.

Seven

But for the mark on his forehead, she would never have recognized him.

He was older, of course, as all of them were older; and deeply tanned from the nomadic life God had given him. The tension and grief she'd read on his face as she'd packed his supplies for travel were now etched deeply, indelibly, on every feature.

All this, she might have anticipated. But there was more. Even beneath the tan, she saw a redness of nose . . . which spoke of too much wine. And in his eyes, once so like hers, she read a disturbing expression. Was it cruelty? Bitterness? Cynicism? Or something more?

His voice, at once heavy with remembered pain and shallow, shied away from certain subjects—as when she'd marveled at the size of his group, still at some distance, and said, "My son, God has blessed you richly."

He'd scarcely nodded, brusquely, as though the collection of chattering youngsters and slim, graceful young men and women meant nothing to him.

And yet later, when he'd brought his favorite son to meet her, his voice had vibrated with pride. "Enoch, my son," he said, "for whom I named my city."

"A city!" Then he had done well, despite the curse.

He shrugged deprecatingly. "Not such a city as yours," he said. "Such would be impossible, when we are cursed to wander . . . Yet it gives us a place of some stability. A place for returning. The women, sometimes, require that."

She yearned to ask if the ground, which had been cursed for his sake, was cursed also for his young.

But there was no need. She saw the wonder with which the children studied the fields and orchards, the amazement with which they knelt to touch a cabbage head, the excitement with which they plucked the swollen fruit of the plum trees and savored it.

Her heart ached for them.

They sat on benches beneath the shade of locust trees. Her children, who had regarded the strangers with quiet curiosity at first, had quickly decided that though dress and complexion, differed interests were the same. Chattering shrilly, they led their young visitors at a run from one point of interest to another. Cain, his expression unreadable, watched.

"Have you been well, my son?" she asked.

Beyond him, she could see Adam approaching, but slowly. Was he uncertain about these guests because he didn't know who they might be? Or because he knew?

"I have been well," Cain answered, adding, "as well as I could expect to be, under God's curse."

She sighed. So many years to nourish his anger, his pain. "Cain—"

He raised an eyebrow, almost challengingly, and waited.

"Can you not find some joy?"

"Joy?" he asked tightly. "I found joy in tilling the earth and watching it produce young green, watching it ripen under my care to golden grain. To fruit." He spread his hands, palms up. "Once, my fingers were stained with earth and growing things. No matter how much I washed them, scouring them with sand, still they wore the color of soil."

She remembered.

"Now when I plant a seed, it shrivels. When I reach to pluck fruit from a tree in passing, it recoils from me."

He thrust his face forward. "We live in sand. We travel in sand and dust. The taste of dust is forever in our mouths, its dryness in our nostrils. At night, we hear the sound of wind—in sand. In dust. When we walk, there's no softness of grass beneath our feet, no green to relieve our sight. Just—"

"*Cain.*"

He stiffened. Then, after a long moment, he turned with agonizing slowness. "My . . . father." There was the dryness of sand in his voice. He cleared his throat, then slowly slipped to his knees before Adam, pressing his forehead to Adam's feet.

Adam's glance sought Eve's, and she met it, reading there all the old sorrows, the old loves, the old searching.

Gently, then, he pulled Cain erect and kissed him. "Have you been well, my son?"

The caravan settled in a ravine where the stream pooled before reaching the river.

"We will stay only a few days," Cain said. He spoke it like a promise, as though wanting to cause them no trouble. "It is our way—to move on quickly from any campsite."

Meshanath's son Rubin listened in rapt attention, his eyes glowing. His voice broke, as it now had a habit of doing, ascending from near-bass to soprano. "How exciting that must be! Have you seen wider rivers than ours?"

"We have seen the sea."

"The sea! What is this sea like?"

Weaving on a small lap loom, Eve half-listened to Cain's narrative, and remembered what he had been like as a child, so easily hurt. And as a man, how grievously he'd been wounded when his sacrifice was scorned. *Sin lies at the door,* God had said.

Now—responding to Rubin's animation and the attention of the other children, Cain was warm and gentle. But the expressions she had read in the lines of his face and in his eyes on his arrival had spoken more of coldness and brutality. What incidents had carved those lines? What damage had been wrought by grief and guilt, and how much by nourished jealousy and anger?

When she and Adam had been cast from Eden, their emotions, too, had been torn. Some of the scars had taken years to heal. Perhaps some still remained. Most, at least, had lost their power to wound. Adam and she had learned to release what was no longer theirs to hold. They had turned to the life that was.

If only Cain had allowed healing to happen, if he'd turned toward whatever the new life held of hope and happiness . . .

Rubin was asking about the city, now—and Seth, whittling sticks for drumming, smiled. But, Eve thought, Seth's ears were just as alert as his young nephew's. Nearby sat Enoch, his face alight, as he said, "My father has a drum."

"The copper one, still?" Eve asked gently, hoping not to disturb Cain's narrative.

"It *is* copper, my grandmother!" He asked eagerly, "You have seen it?"

She nodded. "He played it during the Creation Hymn, while Ab—" she stopped mid-word "—while his brother played other instruments."

Apparently, he hadn't noticed her near-slip. "He plays it still," said Enoch. "And sometimes I play it, too."

"For the Creation Hymn?" she asked.

He frowned.

Her heart sank. Surely, of all the things she had ever expected of him, Cain would have respected that parting wish.

But perhaps they called it by another name! "A poem," she said, leaning forward. "A long poem about Creation—about the world, and how God made it."

"Which god?" he asked.

She wanted to draw him close, to compensate for what he had lost. "Surely," she said, forcing her voice to an evenness, "surely your father has told you of the beginning of the world?"

Cain had heard. "When I left here, Mother," he said in soft, cold tones, "I left behind . . . certain beliefs."

Adam said, "You haven't neglected the worship of God!"

"I was cursed from His presence, you'll remember."

"Oh, Cain—"

"So were we," said Adam. "When He expelled us from Eden, it seemed we had lost Him, as well as our home. And the earth was turned against us."

"Still, it bears for you. Your work is required. But it *bears.*"

Adam cleared his throat before continuing. Perhaps he had heard, as she had, Eve thought, the depths of Cain's despair, betrayed by that single word.

"Perhaps the earth *doesn't* bear for you in this same way. But I saw your flocks—"

"Scrawny, from lack of rich forage."

"Still, they grow, my son. And multiply."

"We have the wool, true. A poorer grade than yours. But our women do make cloth." He shrugged. "For food, there is little but bone."

"There are the fruits of the trees."

"The dates, true. The figs in their season." His voice grayed with grief. "But surely you can see the difference between what you have here, and what we know as nomads!"

Adam said hesitantly, "For that, I have only what you tell me. But I know the difference between Eden and what we have here. And I know that God is still with us, that the same God who made Eden, and who made this land we till, also made the places where you dwell. That He moves there, as well—in the night breeze, in the streams—"

"What few there are," Cain interjected coldly.

Adam went on, as before. "His blessing is with you in the fruit of the womb." His glance touched Enoch, and Cain flinched. "He will speak to you—as He does to us. He is the God of all, my son," Adam finished softly. "And whether or not His face seems turned from you, yours must be turned toward Him."

"Please, Cain," Eve said softly. But she had pled with him before.

He shrugged.

The silence stretched. Throbbed. Suffocated.

Then Rubin whispered longingly, "You were talking about the sea . . ."

Despite Cain's reticence, there was celebration. *How could there not be,* Eve wondered, *with this sudden introduction of so many who share our blood and features?*

Certainly, Cain's family were tanned darkly. Their skin gleamed with applications of oils and creams, which to Eve condensed the aromas of exotic desert flowers she would never see. But in their eyes and expressions, she could read echoes of the past and duplications of the present. She smiled to recognize elements of her own children in these young strangers, who danced with abandon, whether music was played or not. Their leaps and twirls seemed dictated by their own high spirits, their enchantment with grass and abundant water.

Never had she heard such music—flaring, rippling, soaring, melting, insisting that hands drop work so that feet might join the frolic.

Never had she tasted such food—far spicier than hers, igniting a pleasant fire on her tongue, warming her throat and—it seemed—her whole body. And the women of Cain's tribe seemed as delighted with Eve's dishes. They didn't declare them bland at all, but rather cooling, soothing.

She shared her recipes with them, as they shared theirs—pressing into her hands small packets of herbs and spices, and training her in their uses. Describing how they cooked over open fires, kept alive despite sand-weighted winds, they warmed their hands at her oven, shaking their heads not with jealousy, but in awe.

She could love these people, Eve knew, with a sinking heart, already anticipating their departure. She felt especially drawn to Karime, a lithe, lovely young woman whose lilting spirit seemed incapable of containment. Her eyes glowed. Her lips seemed always to verge on laughter. Each soft word spoke caring, and her smooth fingertips seemed always reaching to touch, to pat, to comfort, to encourage.

Cain sat apart from the festivities, which lasted long into the night. The children danced until they dropped, then draped themselves wherever they happened to be, their breathing deep and peaceful. The adults remained long past yawning, listening to music of instruments and chanting voices. Eve knew a quality of sharing past description, and held her breath in hope as Adam, at last, invited everyone to join at the altar, for the Creation Hymn.

At first, it seemed they would. Then Cain cleared his throat—nothing more—and, without even turning, the strangers shook their heads. Eve shivered. Closeness had evaporated. They were two camps, now—separated by downcast eyes and nervous movements, and a haste to be gone from the place of sharing.

Only Karime paused to offer explanation. Her fingertips touched Eve's shoulder gently. "It is only," she said sadly, "that we have our own gods, and they would be offended."

And then, as softly as breath, she, too, was gone. Only Cain remained, his face rigid, to bid them good night.

In the quiet hush of morning, Eve prepared meal for cakes. Still yawning, Arusha laid a plate of figs and dates, fresh plums and sliced cheeses, and Durel turned the lamb, which had been roasting, slowly, through the night. God had slowed the flow of children for Adam and Eve, but always there were young faces glowing with promise, young voices questioning, young hands to help.

And as the young claimed the present, the older children melted into memory.

Eve had asked Cain about Sael, and he had answered stiffly, "She lies buried in the land of Nod, east of Eden, where I first went from here." Before Eve could ask if she had died soon after their leaving, or how she had died, or if any of the children who swelled the caravan had been hers, he was gone. He'd returned much later, with Adam and the other men, but he carefully avoided her eyes.

Trying to sleep that night, holding herself still that she might not waken Adam, she thought of Sael.

Sael had never dwelt as deeply in Eve's heart as had many of the others. Perhaps because she'd been bigger, because she'd seemed so self-sufficient. Perhaps because she had given to Cain the loyalty most daughters reserved for their mothers.

And now she was dead. And had been, . . . perhaps for many years.

Tears started in Eve's eyes.

All those years, when she'd thought of Cain and grieved for him and for Abel, it had seldom occurred to her to be concerned for Sael. *Forgive me,* she prayed into the night. And she wasn't certain whether it was to God she prayed, or to the spirit of Sael.

True to his promise, Cain left on the third day.

The dew, dropped by the mist that rose each night, lay thick on the grass. Cain bent to touch it, then prostrated himself to the ground, allowing it to soak his face, his beard, his clothing. He made no comment, nor did anyone else dare to do so. On his face, Eve recognized that youthful grief he had shown on leaving once before, and a bitter hatred grown old in the years between.

Eve's eyes misted as the women bowed and offered gifts—vials of oil and spices and carved stone jars of the flower-scented creams. But her tears over-flowed as Karime caught her in a tight embrace and sobbed her sorrow at leaving.

Love, as she had felt it for the closest of her daughters, forced a prayer from her swirling thoughts. *Please, let this one stay.*

"It is better that she goes." God's words filled her mind.

I will teach her of you, her thoughts pleaded.

"You would try."

Releasing Karime, Eve sighed. Had it been imagination, or had God's sigh preceded hers? "I love you, my child," she said, "and will pray our

God's blessing on you each day. Now, dry your eyes. And go with your people . . ."

They walked beside Cain's caravan as it turned toward town.

Cain would trade furs and woolen cloth, he explained, for metals. Perhaps for a water pot or two, if they were reasonable in price. And the women, he'd said drily, would surely want to buy cosmetics. And ornaments for their ears and ankles.

Eve was always amazed at how quickly the town grew. Like a giant insect, it reached farther and farther into the arable land. There were three wells, now, to serve it. And even then, she'd been told, the lines of women waiting to fill their water pots were sometimes long and impatient.

Trying to lessen the grief of parting, she scanned the homes they passed. The newer dwellings, on the outskirts, seemed larger than earlier buildings. The walls shone with newness. From some entryways, plants grew in hanging pots, and flowers brightened some dooryards. Color was everywhere: in the flowers, in the woven-work hanging behind windows or doorways, in the clothing of laughing girls.

But, even more than the color, she noticed the sound. It murmured and bubbled and flowed and burst out in freshets of laughter. There were the sounds of animals, working and grazing, the chatter of children, a bright staccato against the complaining of men who shared a wineskin at the base of a wall.

She heard the sounds of hammers on wood, of metal on metal. The slap of clay to a wooden slab. The shushing of shuttles plying their patterns among vibrant yarns. The scuffling of playing children. Women shaking dusty rugs to the breeze. Pots scraping on stone, or thumping to wooden tables. She heard the sound of bread being kneaded, of knives slicing through food—

It seemed, if she shut her eyes, that she could hear all the sounds of the city, mingled, weaving a medley at once melodious and grating.

Then, gradually, as they moved along a dusty street, as they approached a group of people, the sounds seemed to part in silence. Movement ceased, except for an uneasy following of eyes grown suddenly thoughtful.

Eve glanced at Adam. He'd noticed, too.

The disquietude was caused by more than the intrusion of an unusually large caravan. It concerned more than the appearance of strangers. The city had burgeoned so swiftly that strangers might be found living only streets away. With sudden certainty, Eve recognized the reason:

Cain's mark.

And she could tell by Cain's expression, at once wary and weary, that he'd met the reaction before.

A muttering rose from a small group of boys. Three stooped to the street, selecting stones. The first young arm drew back to throw.

Though Cain never flinched, Eve did.

There was no need. Quickly, men moved to pinion the youth's arm to his side. They spoke quickly. Urgently. The boys stiffened, their stones dropping to the dust. One bowed in apology, then fled. The others, mumbling, turned deliberately, busying themselves with a game of dice.

The scene replayed itself, with variations, a dozen times before Cain had made his purchases, turned back the way they'd come, and ridden into the distance.

Karime's parting embrace still a pressure on her shoulders, her kiss a warmth tears could never erase, Eve watched until the caravan was like a marching row of ants, and then until it disappeared. Until she saw on the horizon only a wavering, which might still have been their movement, or might have been rising heat. Or only her imagination.

Adam touched her arm, and she moved with him toward home. The children, just as silent, walked beside them. Seth's expression was set in thoughtful lines. Rubin, morose, kicked pebbles from his path.

Eve felt fresh tears gather in her eyes.

He was gone. Again.

The pain she felt on this parting was duller than the agony of the earlier separation. But it was more hopeless, as well. Before, he'd taken with him the knowledge of all he'd learned at home. And he'd taken the Hymn.

The Hymn was gone, now, Cain's godless children growing without ever having repeated it.

God had banished Cain and turned the earth against him. But Cain had inflicted far greater damage against himself.

He'd banished God.

Years passed, with no further word from Cain. Eve's prayers for his family, especially for Karime, continued, but her tears had long since dried. Whenever she smoothed the fragrant cream on a child's injury, or experimented with a pinch of spices, she was warmed by remembrance.

Sometimes, though, townspeople who'd traveled a great distance told tales of a man with a strange mark on his forehead. A man who, though he'd committed some great sin against a god, had that god's protection.

"Cain," Adam would say. "Our firstborn Cain, who murdered his brother, Abel."

But heads would shake. "No. No. This man is different. I never saw him, but I was told by someone who has that he is taller than most men."

"And dark," another would add, while the first head shook in affirmation.

"Dark from life in the desert," Adam would insist.

"Dark. With strange powers."

"He snatches men's speech from their tongues, so that they never speak again!"

"He has been known—" this in hushed tones "to kill men with one glance of his eyes."

"There have been those who tried to kill him."

"Who lay in wait as he passed."

"But whoever flung the spear—"

"Or threw the stone—"

"Or tried in any way to strike him down—"

"That man would die in some horrible way. Always—some *unnatural* way."

Adam would try again, patiently: "God said that whoever should kill Cain would be punished seven times—"

"But no one has killed him, I tell you! Many have tried, but that god protects him."

"*Our* God, the *only* God, protects *Cain*," Adam would explain. "He placed the mark upon his forehead for his protection—"

Muttering, shaking their heads, the others would turn away.

"The son of Adam?" one might be heard to say. "No man such as that one could have sprung from Adam!"

Occasionally, travelers on camels might bring word of a city of huts made of grass and wood slabs, of leaning wooden structures inhabited by wild animals, chased from their homes only when a fierce nomadic tribe rested from its travels . . .

One day, many years past Cain's visit, three young men inquired in the sprawling city where the man Adam might live.

"A magnificent city!" exclaimed one as they took refreshment from the hands of Eve and Ralisha, a lovely, docile daughter with shy eyes and easily roused color, at full-bloom then. "Never have we seen such a city as yours!"

Eve smiled gently at Adam. They didn't count the city "theirs"—they had, in fact, moved three times to escape its expanding borders.

"Where is your home?" asked Adam.

One gestured, his smiling glance enveloping the blushing girl. "In the land of Nod, near the city of Enoch."

Adam's hand stiffened on the plate of dates Ralisha had offered him. "My son Cain's city!"

Eve's hands fumbled the bowl of bread and cheeses. "Is our son well?"

One hastily swallowed his drink before answering, "It is because of him that we come."

Eve moved unsteadily to stand behind Adam. She grasped his shoulder. His hand reached to cover hers.

"He is still well. . . ." The man's tone robbed the words of reassurance.

"He seldom speaks," one said. "He has grown old."

The anger, thought Eve. *The anger and the bitterness have congealed within him, like hardening clay.*

"I am Mehujael," said the oldest, "the son of Irad, who was born of Enoch, the son of Cain."

The son of Adam, Eve finished, in her thoughts.

"And these are my younger brothers, Aren and Thusa." He paused, while introductions were acknowledged, then continued: "There are times when the father of my father's father suffers great agony of spirit, when he cries aloud in his sleep."

"There are times," interjected Aren—with difficulty, it seemed, forcing his eyes to relinquish Ralisha—"when he speaks of his brother's murder."

"And of the vengeance of one of his gods."

"The only God," said Adam.

There was a slight silence.

"Perhaps. And at these times, when his spirit is troubled, he tries to recall a . . . a . . ."

"A *hymn!*" Eve blurted. Then, embarrassed, she turned aside.

Adam reached to draw her back. "The Creation Hymn," he said.

Thusa grinned, startlingly white teeth glistening against his sun-darkened skin. "Yes! He called it that!"

" 'In the beginning,' " Adam began, " 'God created the heaven and the earth.' "

If it were possible, Thusa's grin broadened. He nodded energetically.

Aren smiled dazzlingly at Ralisha, as though she alone were responsible for this agreement.

Shyly, she flicked a sober glance toward him and moved, with subtle grace, into the house.

He sighed eloquently. Eve, observing, suppressed a chuckle.

Mahujael was saying, "The later words avoid him. He remembers a line or two here and there, but there are large gaps, and his anger increases." He sighed. "It was the hope of my father's father that you could give us these words."

Eve drew a long breath of thanksgiving. God—who had cast Cain out of his homeland, who had turned the land against him and cursed him to a life of wandering—God was still nudging Cain's mind, forcing him to acknowledge that a tie existed. *Thank you,* she breathed within her.

As it did whenever she prayed, peace formed within her.

Adam spoke simply, but she knew that his heart must be stirred as well. They'd often spoken of their shared sorrow that Cain had turned from God. "We will be happy to teach you the Hymn," he said. "You will be able to stay with us for some days?"

The young men nodded, almost—Eve thought, hiding her smile—in unison, as though they'd practiced. Aren, watching the doorway with avid attention, seemed to have gained additional incentive.

"I will prepare lodging," Eve said, and excused herself.

Once within the house, she called Rynadab. "My son," she said, "run and find your brother Seth. Make certain that he joins us tonight for the Hymn."

Only then, pondering the possible effects of Aren's open admiration, did she seek Ralisha for help with the linens.

Ralisha had seldom been difficult to read. Like a shy doe, she often closed her feelings within those lowered eyes, her head bent carefully to further shield her thoughts. But color was hard to hide, and hers was flaming. Throbbing in her cheeks. Glowing along her neck, where a pulse beat visibly.

Eve ventured, "They seem fine young men. Polite. Well-taught."

Ralisha smoothed a cushion. "Manners can be like a salve, applied where needed."

Eve hid her smile. Ralisha should have been a son. Such wisdom would go far in bargaining. "I thought the youngest handsome. Didn't you?"

"And which was he?" So casually.

"The gold-robed one."

"Oh, *yes!*" Ralisha's subtlety had fled. She dropped the linens, launching herself against Eve's bosom, knocking them both off balance, against the wall.

Eve held her, stroking with gentle hands the slender shoulders. Her heart thumped heavily. *Poor child. Poor child. If she should show this clearly how she feels—*

"When he looked at me," Ralisha whispered. "Did you see how his eyes—" She pulled away, as though to study Eve's expression. "His glance was *tangible!* I felt it, gently, on me. Not like the eyes of the city men, ripping and raking." She shuddered. "But I could feel his glance, like fingertips, stroking me." She hugged herself as though to still a quivering.

"He found you beautiful," said Eve. *And no wonder,* she thought. *No wonder.*

"I had to leave," Ralisha paused. "I was afraid."

The whitewashed walls shone cleanly in late sunlight, and a shadow of breeze-tossed vine made fragile etchings across their surface. Eve turned Ralisha toward her. "This is your father's house. You needn't fear. No stranger dare touch you here, against your wishes."

"But if I *wish* his touch?" Her cheeks paled, swiftly. "If what I fear is . . ." With a touchingly dramatic gesture, she dropped her fingertips to her breast. "My mother!" She held Eve close. "What can you say to help me when I fear myself?"

Gently, Eve set her apart again, but Ralisha tugged her back. "Send me on an errand. Somewhere distant!"

Eve smiled. "You'd hate me."

She nodded. "Yes. But better to hate you . . . than myself."

They worked together within the house until it was essential there be water brought fresh from the well.

Ralisha listened at the doorway. Peered from the window.

Eve said comfortably, "The men will be off somewhere, visiting flocks or bins of grain."

Ralisha pressed a finger to her lips, listened again, then lifted the water pot and left with swift and silent steps.

Smiling, Eve watched from the doorway.

But her smile congealed as she saw the young man detach himself from a shadowed corner of the porch, and follow. Her heart thudded as briskly as though she were the one being sought. She could imagine Ralisha's expression as she turned with the water pot half-filled and saw him there. *Don't drop the pot,* she thought. It was one Adam, after long consideration, had bought from a local potter, only because he himself had been unable to achieve such size and sturdiness.

They were out of sight. She imagined their emotions—these two young people, with blood running hot in their veins. With a need for love and being needed strong in both of them. With the additional appeal of unknowns. Two young strangers, from vastly different cultures. So much to multiply their mutual attraction!

Her thoughts more with them than on what she did, she arranged cheese and ripe olives on a plate.

What did she know of him, anyway, this handsome stranger? As Ralisha had said, manners could be a salve, a cosmetic.

Deliberately, she halved a pear.

She must trust Ralisha.

But Ralisha had expressed distrust of herself.

And she was fragile. What chance would she have, if he should try to ravish her?

He was a kinsman.

*Every*one was a kinsman. And evil abounded.

But he had come on an errand from Cain.

Swiftly, Eve snatched a smaller water pot and rushed toward the spring, making no effort to be quiet.

Despite her sound, they clearly hadn't heard her. There could have been a stampede of oxen, she was sure, and they'd have been unaware. The water pot lay shattered near the spring. Eve knew a moment of personal pain. It had taken years for Adam to bring himself to such a purchase.

Ralisha and Aren stood apart, but leaning slightly toward one another. Ralisha's lips were parted, her color ebbing and flowing, that betrayer pulse evident even at some distance. Her glance held his. And he, absorbed so totally that Eve's heart ached equally for both, seemed more smitten than any young man she'd ever watched before.

Guilty at watching, she quietly backed away.

They seemed so vulnerable, the two of them, drinking of one another's beauty with their eyes. And full of yearning. In her loins, she felt an echo of that yearning, as she had known it for Adam, over and over again.

She paused.

Sunlight threw dappling shadows over them. A breeze caressed Ralisha's hair, and Aren reached tenderly to smooth it back. Then, lightly, his fingertips stroked her cheek. And moaning, she leaned still farther toward him. Swiftly, he caught her, capturing her lips, pulling her close. Her body arched to meet his.

Eve moved closer, by a step.

And then, still tenderly, he set her from him.

Relieved, Eve backed away three cubits' length. Then stopped.

A new intensity had gathered in Aren's glance, a new tension in his stance. Eve read the effects in Ralisha's heightened color. She poised, almost on tiptoe, partially turned as though to escape . . . yet one hand reached ever so slowly toward his face.

And her eyes. Pleading. *Pleading for what?* Eve wondered. That his love might transform her, carrying her forever beyond childhood's strictures? Or that he might leave her—still, for a little while—in the safety of innocence?

In Eve's veins pulsed an echo of Ralisha's ambivalence. She pressed fingertips to the hollow of her throat, as though to still the sounds of beating heart and surging blood.

And then, with eloquent simplicity, Aren claimed Ralisha's hand and raised it to his lips.

And when at last Ralisha nodded, Eve knew—as thoroughly as she knew temptation and the ease with which it victimized—that she must intervene. She clattered ahead with exaggerated sound. Pretending not to notice Ralisha's swift confusion or Aren's blush, she set about filling the smaller water pot.

"Ah!" she said, not looking at them, but hearing movement—at last, relaxing tension. "So the old water pot finally broke, did it? I'd thought there was a crack forming. A shame! It was a fine pot, for as long as I've had it."

When she turned, the smaller water pot filled three times over, Aren was gone. Ralisha, smiling dreamily, stooped to give Eve a quick and tender kiss.

But she could not always rush in with a dusty water pot to save her daughter's virginity. And the young men were to be there . . . how many endless days?

Seth and Enos returned with Rynadab.

Enos, scarcely seven years old, followed his father as closely as Meshanath had once trailed Seth. Eve thought warmly of Meshanath, who'd carried his near-idolatry into manhood, and in every way tried to imitate his older brother. Although he farmed a distant valley, as often as possible he gathered his family and traveled by oxcart to spend time with Seth and his growing tribe.

Adam rose from his seat, beaming approval, as Seth entered the room where visitors rested on cushions, waiting for the evening meal. "My son," he said. "My son, Seth."

As Eve oversaw the preparations of the meal, she thought of Adam's prophecy, that Seth would be a special son. *Surely* it was Seth God had meant when He'd mentioned the Seed of the Woman! From that long-ago Seventh Day when they'd found the children worshiping through music, this "special" son had grown increasingly involved with worship. Although he tilled his land with more than usual fervor and tended healthy flocks, each day found him with some small group of men or other, in prayer and discussion.

"For far too long," he would say, "we've put distance between God and ourselves. Too few of us gather even for the Creation Hymn, teaching it to our children. Too few of us burn offerings. And when we do, too often we do it in fear, afraid to send up our voices, as well as the smoke of fat lambs. Why should we fear the God Who made us? *Why?* His caring is evident all about us. In the bounty we reap from the earth; in the fruit of the womb. It is unfitting that we remain silent, when even the birds of the air daily sing His praises. *We* must sing out to Him! *Cry* out to Him!"

Adam's introductions pulled Eve from her thoughts.

"My son," he was saying, "these are the grandsons of your nephew Enoch. You remember Enoch, who came with your brother Cain."

"Of course." Seth moved quickly forward, embracing each of the young men as his name was pronounced.

"They have come," Adam said with great satisfaction, "to learn about our God."

Mehujael raised a hand in disagreement. "We have come only to learn the hymn," he said. "My grandfather feels that it might soothe his father's spirit."

Seth settled easily onto a cushion. "To learn the Creation Hymn *is* to learn about our God. To learn, at least, how He fashioned the heavens and the earth. And"—he smiled toward his father and mother—"and how He created man."

Mahujael bowed his head deferentially, yet his hand remained raised slightly in protest. "Forgive me, but I have heard the myth of which you speak."

Eve drew a deep, startled breath, but Seth shot her a look both of warning and comfort.

"It is not a myth, but fact."

Thusa snickered. It was Mahujael's turn to discipline with a glance.

"Forgive me, my uncle," Thusa said, addressing Seth, and nodded as well toward Adam. "Forgive me, my grandfather's grandfather. It is only that—"

"We are nomads, it is true," interjected Mahujael, "but we are also men of reason."

"As *we* are men of reason," Seth pursued. "Look about you—how the years evolve in seasons. How each tree knows when to put forth its branch, when to blossom, and when to swell the blossom to mature fruit. Who do you think taught it?"

Thusa made a gesture of annoyance. "It is foolishness to talk of teaching trees! Trees are wood and leaves. Nothing more."

"Then how do you explain the fruit?"

Thusa stood angrily. "We have come on a simple errand—"

"*Thusa*—" warned Mahujael, and his brother sat, crossing his arms in a singularly childlike expression of defiance. His eyes were downcast, his expression sullen.

Eve yearned to spank him, old as he was. Then a stronger emotion overcame her: sorrow that these young men knew nothing of God. Her glance touched Aren, whose thoughts were obviously elsewhere.

But Seth, she thought proudly. *Seth will teach them.*

He tried.

He spoke all through the meal, cajoling, agreeing whenever possible, reasoning, offering proofs.

But each proof they discarded as fancy, each part of the Creation account as myth.

Before they adjourned to the clearing for the nightly ritual, Eve knew that the young men would strive to learn the poem only because it might humor an old man. They would take none of it to their hearts; their hearts were closed.

What have you done, Cain? she grieved.

She knew the answer all too well. Out of his anger and bitterness, he had raised up a godless nation.

Suddenly, though the night was warm, she trembled, wondering what that might mean for the future of the whole race.

"It is good," Seth was proclaiming, while the crowd sat hushed and eager. "It is good for us to cry out to the God who made us!"

"Hear us, we pray!" The voices of the crowd swelled. "Hear us as we cry out to you, our God!"

Hear us, Eve continued in her heart. *Touch the hearts of these young men.*

But they sat through the litany with expressions that proved their continued unbelief. And Eve's spirit knew an agony that intensified as she realized the possible impact on Ralisha.

Ralisha and Aren had parted from the group as they returned to the house.

Eve searched the distant shadows, but without result. Ralisha would have to guard herself. From what she'd observed of the young man, Eve didn't really think that he would take her against her will.

Heart sinking, she suspected that he wouldn't need to.

Heavily, she attended to the needs of their guests, and when Adam asked why Ralisha wasn't helping, she simply shrugged.

Discussion plodded on, Seth forming his pleas in many different ways; the two strangers parrying each verbal thrust.

And then, from the shadows, Eve heard the two low voices, and knew relief. Surely, there hadn't been time. . . . One look at Ralisha's face assured her. There was no shame written there, only the glow of happiness she'd hoped to read, one day.

Aren's face, as well, communicated joy. With reluctance, it seemed, he released Ralisha's hand, and bowed before Adam. "I would ask for your daughter in marriage," he said.

The problem of multiple gods would be a difficult one, Ralisha herself pointed out to her parents. They talked quietly, after the guests had retired to their room. She and Aren had spoken of that. And, while he seemed as adamant as she in his beliefs, he had promised not to intrude on her worship.

"Perhaps in time," she said, "I can convince him that our God is the only God."

"Perhaps," said Adam, but without conviction.

"And I know that I'll be far away." She caught their hands. "And I'll miss you desperately. But—"

"But you love him," Eve supplied.

"I love him. *Yes!*"

"For this," recited Adam, "shall a son—or a daughter—leave mother and father—"

She has been such a special daughter, Eve thought. *As all of them were special.*

"We will be married," she said, "before we leave. In two days."

In only two days, thought Eve. The time, which had seemed interminable, now seemed not nearly enough, even for goodbyes.

In the morning, holding Ralisha's hand as though it were a fragile treasure, Aren agreed that there could be a ceremony of sorts before they left. "But there are certain prescribed rituals, as well, when we get home," he said. "Only then, can we be *fully* joined."

Ralisha settled closer, within the curve of his arm.

Eve had a feeling that whatever he might suggest, she would only smile and nod.

"We must speak to my father, of course," he continued. "And we must approach some older relatives—my aunts, and grandmothers. And we must, most particularly, present you to Narice."

"Narice," repeated Eve. "A lovely name."

"Is he a relative, too?" Ralisha asked.

"She," corrected Aren. And there was just the slightest pause before he added, "She is my senior wife."

It was a practice, Mahujael explained later—quietly, to Adam and Eve—embraced by some of his kinsmen. "Because of the nomadic life," he explained, "it is sometimes more work than one woman can perform, to tend to the children and the food, the setting-up of tents . . ." His voice trailed off, and he sighed. "It is another cultural difference of which we should, surely, have been aware."

When Adam did not answer, he continued, "I can understand your reluctance to give your daughter into what seems to you an impossible union—even though I see my brother's pain."

"Our daughter suffers, as well," Adam said stiffly.

"I have seen that. I have seen their deep love for one another."

Quietly, Eve disengaged herself from the conversation and went to find Ralisha. But there was no comfort that she could offer. Nevertheless, she said, "This sadness will pass, my daughter."

Ralisha merely shook her head, and Eve, rising sadly and going to the garden to gather herbs, questioned the truth of her own pronouncement.

Two additional nights, the brothers listened intently to the words of the Creation Hymn, committing them to memory. During the day, they recited the words passionlessly, allowing Adam to correct them where they'd erred.

Aren—more wooden than the others in expression, his eyes haunted by pain—seemed nevertheless the most accurate in his recital. The morning they readied themselves to leave, he took Eve aside and kissed her hand. "Please know," he said, "that I would not willingly have brought this pain to your house."

She nodded, reassuring him.

"And know that the pain with which I return to my own house will never ease." His voice broke. "Never."

Impulsively, she covered his hands with hers. "All pain dims with time," she said.

"Not this."

Embarrassed to be a witness to such raw grief, she turned toward the others, but he restrained her.

"Pray for me," he said awkwardly. "Pray to this god you worship, as I will pray to all of mine, that the love I have been denied will not turn my love for Narice to hatred."

"I will pray," she promised, "both for you and for Narice."

He nodded stiffly, and was gone.

As she watched them from sight, her heart was heavy. If their errand brought peace to Cain, she should surely be grateful for their coming.

But all she could think of was Ralisha, sodden with tears, her grace and her joy corroded, perhaps forever.

You continue to hurt us, my son, she thought.

Part III

Eight

Eve eased herself from the kneading board and sat slumped, breathing heavily. Ayra, weaving in the nearby shade of the vine trained from pillar to pillar, looked up, concern etching a furrow between her eyes.

She's getting old, Eve thought, with the surprise of first discovery. *This daughter, too, is getting old.*

Ayra's once-heavy black hair was thin and graying, her face criss-crossed by wrinkles.

And I am even older. There was the real surprise: that she and Adam were old. In her heart and in her mind, she felt as young as ever—indeed, younger than she had those terrible months after Abel's murder, or when Deri had died in childbirth, or when she had learned that Sael was dead, or when Ralisha's heart was broken. Younger than she had when, just a few short years ago, they had learned of Cain's death.

She had wondered, then, if his great-grandsons had remembered the Hymn and taken it to him, intact, and if it had been of comfort to him. How long it had been—well over four hundred years, at least—since they'd come asking for it to ease his anguish. In all that time, had Cain turned his heart to God? Or continued in his bitterness? From all she had heard of him—through periodic caravans of traders, who sometimes sought Adam, and so left the more lucrative track from the nearby city—the tribe still grew in godless disarray.

But, then, she thought, and sighed deeply, *the nearby city also reeks with evil.* Despite Adam's warnings; despite the way Seth and Enoch and many of his other descendants continued to call on the name of the Lord, and encouraged all to do so.

Warmly, Eve thought of Enoch.

It was strange that the same name could cover Cain's evil city and this godly descendant through Seth's line. Ever since his birth, he'd shown goodness, but—since the birth of Methusaleh—he walked always in a Godly way. Never showing anger, or frustration. Always speaking and acting as though God stood at his shoulder. Or better than that. Perhaps it was Enoch, rather than Seth, that God had—

"Mother!" Ayra's tone indicated that this wasn't the first time she'd called.

"Yes, my daughter." Eve struggled to produce a smile.

"Are you . . . well?"

She nodded. "Of course. Only old. Very, very old."

"And with child again!" Ayra's voice sharpened with disapproval. She herself had left off bearing a hundred years or more before.

Eve smiled. Her own flow of children had slowed to a trickle. This was the first in twenty years, since Ranuel's birth, and fifty years had separated him from Osanti. "If God sees fit to send the children, still—"

Ayra raised a cynical eyebrow. "There is one way to stop their coming!"

Eve ignored that. Adam and she had spoken often of their continuing love for one another, and of their ability, still, to express that love. It had been one of God's richest gifts. They wouldn't deny it.

Ayra's voice was soft once more. "I worry about you."

"I know." She reached to cover Ayra's hand. "You have been a great blessing to me—to *us*—my daughter."

Despite her slowed movements, Ayra still served as midwife to hundreds of women each month, and when a child was lost, or a mother, it became her own personal grief.

The two women shared long moments of companionable silence. Ayra's shuttle clicked rhythmically, and Eve simply sat, eyes half-closed, thoughts half-formed.

Beyond the flowering vine, the summer day evolved as summer days had always passed. Flocks spoke, their voices muted by distance and the slow pace of the afternoon. The slight breeze that stirred the vine sang through the foliage of towering trees. Insects whizzed and whirred, but in slow motion. And at a distance, but drawing closer, Eve could hear Adam's deep tones, and Ranuel's voice . . . raised in anger? Again?

Sighing, she returned to the kneading-board.

Ayra shook her head in sympathy. "He reminds me so much of our twelfth child, Nun. Always so full of *fire!*"

"And yet a good son."

"Now, yes." She chuckled. "Now that the coals of the fire are banked by age."

"And maturity," Eve added. More than anything he might imagine he required, Ranuel needed maturity. He needed direction for his considerable enthusiasm. Adam had tried to channel his energies, giving him responsibility and many freedoms.

"Ranuel, too, is a good young man," Ayra was saying. "I remember so well his birth, the energy with which he came—as though he couldn't wait to begin life."

Eve nodded. That was it, exactly. Ranuel was always bursting to begin. To touch. To taste. To see. To experience.

"Once he and Tarelle are married . . ."

Eve thought of the gentle girl, so obviously in love with this brash young man. Her own personality so subdued. So sweet. Eve had often feared that Ranuel was wrong for her; that he would hurt her. She'd mentioned her fears for this tender great-granddaughter to Seth.

"He'll be fine," Ayra affirmed. Her shuttle increased speed, as though the subject were decided.

But the argument beyond the vine, beyond the herb garden and fowl pens, was obviously not yet decided. At least not to the satisfaction of Adam, whose voice, also, was raised.

Eve dropped the dough to the board, wiped her hands down the sides of her linen robe, and went to see for herself what this new crisis might be.

We should have borne Ranuel, she thought ruefully, *while we were still young enough to match his shouting.*

He stood with his hands on his hips, his head thrust forward, his feet braced so firmly that his strong young calf muscles bulged and glowed beneath his sweat-shiny tan. Her heart turned. How beautiful he was! If Adam and she had produced in him a fiery rebel, they'd also borne a man without blemish. She'd seen how the girls in the city ravished him with their eyes, and had counted it fortunate that—so far—he'd had eyes and heart only for Tarelle.

Adam was saying, "—only evil. All we've trained you to shun. The gambling, the harlots—"

"If you've trained me well, need you worry?" His tone was impertinent, his head tilted to one side.

He should, Eve knew, have a slap to the face for that. But Adam only sighed with weariness.

Perhaps Ayra was right, she thought heavily. Perhaps they *were* too old for more children. Absently, she dropped her hands to the bulge below her waist. Or where her waist had been.

"There are still the sheep in the east pen to be sheared—"

"I'll do them when I come home. Or tomorrow morning."

"Tomorrow morning, we mend the gate—"

"I'll do both. And I'll do them alone. I'm young and strong—" He raised an arm, forming the muscles into a tight bulge. "I must *live,* my father! The sap of life runs in my veins, and I feel I must burst! I need to see these caravans, these strange men from distant lands! I need to hear their music . . . to let my blood throb with it! I need this as the plants thirst for each night's dew. And I *will have it!*"

Adam reached for his arm, but Ranuel avoided him.

"I would prefer your permission, my father. But, either way, *I am going!*"

Adam lunged for him.

Again, Ranuel danced out of his way.

"Ranuel!" shouted Eve.

From a safe distance, he faced them both, and his tone was milder. "I love you," he said, "but you are old. How can you understand these . . ." Mutely, he touched both hands to his breast in a dramatic gesture, which spoke wrenchingly of youth.

Adam asked angrily, "Do you suppose I haven't felt those same yearnings?"

"But so long ago, my father! The world has changed."

"It is because of that that I forbid your going."

Ranuel's expression hardened. A moment later, he was mounting his blanketed sorrel. Moments beyond that, nothing remained but the dimming patter of hooves.

Eve rested her hand on Adam's arm.

"I must go after him," he sighed.

"Just give me a little time," she said. "I'll change into something clean."

Except for the nature of their errand, the day was perfect for a rest from work.

Their cart moved easily along the dusty road, the donkey's hooves light and dainty, beating a rhythm that echoed in Eve's heart.

Flowers bloomed everywhere. The fields bordering the roadway were rich in them. Her favorite, lacy wild carrot, grew lushly—some stems, taller than her head, were topped by ornate white blossoms larger than platters. A thistle thrust purple bristles of blossom in clusters between her and the clear sky.

Thistles, she thought. God had cursed the earth with them, and yet even His curse showed His love of beauty and detail. Through the years, she had firmed her belief that God was incapable of creating anything that was not good.

It was only people who corrupted.

Her thoughts raced ahead to Ranuel, to what might be happening to him, even then. She'd heard stories of beatings and mutilations. Even of men raping other men.

She shuddered. How could Ranuel approach Tarelle's wedding bed if he had been so violated—

She leaned forward on the seat.

"I've pushed her as fast as she can go," Adam chided gently. His expression proved his worry as deep as hers. His eyes, beneath beetling white brows, were glazed with concern. "He could scarcely be there yet himself."

Within, God's voice whispered, "We must work on this impatience of yours, dear Eve."

She smiled, then realized that He hadn't mentioned Ranuel. *Will all be well?* she pressed.

God sighed, and she thought He whispered, "Eventually."

It was not difficult to find where the caravan circled. As in past years, it had settled in the broad valley of Thorin outside the city, depending on its banners of color and sound to attract the crowds—and on its reputation for gambling, for carousing, for brilliance and music and dancing, for easy and unusual sex . . .

Over the generations, Eve thought, sin had found diverse expressions. Always, it seemed, it had grown a more glamorous façade. More inviting. So few people seemed to find goodness nearly as interesting.

Unwillingly, she reviewed for a moment that seldom-remembered scene in the Garden when sin had corrupted her.

It had seemed so innocent. So unimportant. Perhaps to everyone who first sinned, sin wore that guise.

They left the cart and donkey beneath a spreading locust tree, where there was grass enough for grazing, and hurried toward the sound.

Even outside the boundaries of the carnival, there were movement and sound and temptation. Three costumed youths juggled and tumbled. Girls postured and giggled, jangling their anklets and casting sidelong glances at passing boys. A cluster of men threw dice, imploring the gods of luck to reward them. A young girl, eyes downcast and shivering slightly, was all too evidently the prize.

"Oh, Adam," moaned Eve.

He drew a long, quivering breath and turned aside.

The gamblers turned lazily toward him, their eyes glazed with drinking, mouths twisted into sneers.

Adam pushed Eve slightly behind him, and beckoned to the girl.

She didn't move. It seemed that she couldn't.

"So," one man said appraisingly, "you want her for yourself, do you?"

Another laughed coarsely. "By the look of his old woman's belly, he remembers the game!"

Eve warmed with shame at the short burst of laughter and the brief, lewd examination of their eyes.

"If you throw your money into the pot," one snarled at Adam, "you'll have your chance. If not—" Together, it seemed, they rose into a threatening circle, enclosing him.

Eve walked toward the girl, coaxing, "You could escape, now. There. To the cart! Meet us by the river—"

"No," the child moaned wretchedly. "No. No . . ."

Reluctantly, it seemed, Adam moved away. "Then God protect you," he said gently.

When they were distant enough for speech, he whispered miserably, "If only they'd listen."

She knew. At times, when she could forget her frustration, she knew a soul-deep aching for these sinful people, through whose bloodstreams still coursed her blood and Adam's. If only they'd believe what Adam and Seth and Enoch and young Methusaleh and many others tried to tell them. If only they'd realize that what God had created in love, He might one day destroy in anger.

It seemed so hopeless.

There, not thirty paces from the game they'd left, a young girl offered herself to every man who passed. She was lithe and rather beautiful, in a large-eyed way, but grubby and awkward in her approach. She lacked the ease that experience brought, and she quivered beneath the scorn and insults men hurled at her as they rushed toward the more sophisticated pleasures within the carnival.

Eve spoke to her gently. "Go home to your mother, child." And she went. But probably, Eve knew, just to another site, where she might meet with greater success.

So hopeless.

"No." God spoke again. "Never, never hopeless. They are all your children. And my children."

And yet His words only added to the weight of her sadness.

Once they'd passed the fluttering banners that outlined the world of the caravan, Adam and she might have entered another life. There was the flash of jewelry—silver, gold, copper. The color of vivid cosmetics; of fabrics, dyed to brilliance; of enameled utensils and ornaments. The sounds of timbrels, of cornets and drums.

That was to be expected, Eve thought. These were the descendants of Cain. Memory brought fleeting images carved in gentle pain: young Cain, recognizing imperfection in the flute Adam had carved for him; Cain's drum, its copper polished to near-blazing. And had she not heard long years before that Mahujael's grandson Lamech had, from his polygamous unions, sired two illustrious sons? Jubal, creator of the harp and the organ and many other instruments, who was called by some the father of music. And that other son, Tubalcain, so skilled in intricate metalcraft that he'd instructed others in such arts.

Everywhere she looked, she saw evidence of their increased craft. In the ornaments of caravan-dwellers, in trappings of haughty camels, in booths crowded with enameled trays and copper lamps, with engraved metal head-dresses and girdles, with vases, wall hangings, and intricate fastenings for drapes. Often, Eve had seen such workmanship echoed less expertly in the commerce squares of the nearby city.

Strange foods assaulted her nostrils with rich scents reminiscent of a long-ago gift of spices, from someone she couldn't quite recall . . . and a somehow-related image of carved stone jars, exuding sweet fragrance. She struggled for a moment, striving for recognition, then dismissed the tattered memory for the tangible present.

Everywhere, it seemed, men and women cried in harsh or insinuating voices to sell their wares: rich, soft fabrics ("See, my lady, only touch and consider how sensuously this would glide across your body!"); pottery of every design and color ("Only look, my lady! Would this not beautify your bedroom?"); cosmetics ("See, my lady! Could this not captivate new lovers for your pleasure?")

The scents . . . color caught by the sun through tent hangings and cast to the ground or to already-vivid wares . . . the cajolings of craftsmen and sellers . . . the excitement of those who had come to see, perhaps to buy, but certainly to experience—

Eve found her senses reeling.

Adam hurried her along.

Yes, they must find Ranuel. They must find him before he fell victim to the blandishments of these skilled purveyors of everything from fish to human flesh.

She was nearly dropping with weariness when they saw him at last, standing with a large group of men before a raised platform where a line of dancers swayed to the music of fifes and cymbals.

They danced—sometimes frenziedly, sometimes lazily, but always sensually—their heads draped with transparent fabrics, their eyes surrounded by vivid cosmetics in which fragments of bright metal had been embedded. In their navels glowed jewels, which caught and refracted the light. Their bare arms were olive-toned and supple, inviting in their movements. Bare thighs flashed through parting fabric as their feet moved swiftly, exciting tinkles almost of merriment from the gleaming metal anklets that flowed and clashed and chimed.

One dancer, in the center, moved with the greatest grace. She seemed to flow effortlessly with the music. And the arch of her neck, the movement of her hands, the easy gyrations of her hips and the throbbing of her breasts, all spoke exotic invitation. Temptation. A promise of pleasure beyond speaking.

Eve could only guess at what those movements excited in the veins of the watching men.

And Ranuel.

Ranuel, so unskilled in assessing such promises—having known only the young, awkward adoration of Tarelle's stumbling words and innocent eyes—

They must reach him.

They *must!*

She touched Adam's arm, and he nodded, indicating that he would move forward.

But they were blocked from Ranuel by a sturdy group of bodies—all intent, all unwilling to be moved aside.

All but the central dancer had stepped backward, undulating slightly near the heavy crimson curtain, which screened a wagon or some other large structure. In contrast to their lassitude, she danced with broader movements, with graceful runs and leaps, with joyous twirlings, as she performed alone.

Almost alone.

Through the parting curtain, another figure sprang to the stage. Large. Perhaps a man. But graceful. Eve drew an anguished breath. He wore the scales of a serpent. Over his head was a serpent's head, with glowing eyes and darting, forked tongue.

"There is a myth," said a large man in a tigerskin from the edge of the stage, "about a maiden and a serpent. This myth has come down to us from our father's father's fathers. A beautiful myth, it speaks of that innocence we all have known and lost—much to our pleasure!"

He paused, while applause and laughter sputtered—though all eyes, it seemed to Eve, remained on the dancer. Her movements never faltered, never deteriorated into less than perfect grace.

"It is that myth," the man continued, "which Dartha now portrays."

Eve watched numbly as the dance interpreted her own temptation, though much more sensually than she remembered. Could she, in her innocence, have been so brazen?

A myth, she thought bitterly. All those years, through their careful instruction of their children, through their daily recital of the Creation Hymn, through their pleading and arguing with everyone they met, through their sometimes-frenzied appeals for belief in what they knew to be true. All lost. All diminished to the status of a myth.

She reached to touch Adam. But he withdrew his arm, and she experienced that occasional loneliness grown familiar through their lives together. That total desolation she could feel as he stood within her physical grasp, but alienated by that original sin from any other contact.

Of course. He, too, was watching. He was remembering.

Nor could she close her eyes, divorcing herself from that insistent reenactment of her fall. When she tried, the music remained, and she could visualize still the serpent's coiling, his subtlety, his brilliance and persuasiveness. Better to watch the depiction than to revive within her mind the actual scene.

The serpent dancer offered the fruit, a large, gleaming fruit fashioned of jewels and clay. It glittered and glowed, and Eve's whole being throbbed within her. There was pain where the babe hung, its heaviness multiplied. There was anguish in her throat, her breast, her groin. Her knees sagged ominously.

Don't eat it, her thoughts whispered and surged. *Don't accept the fruit.*

If, by some miracle, the woman on the stage refused the jewelled fruit, time might be thrust backward, and she—Eve—might have another chance . . .

But of course Dartha would accept. She wore the ease of one who had long ago embraced the pleasures of forbidden fruit.

The music had slowed, had grown tender and plaintive. Waiting as Dartha hesitated. Imploring as she examined. Then rising to a frenzy as she accepted and lifted the fruit to her lips.

The dance ended on that frenzy, the instruments climbing to a frantic crescendo. All of the dancers were active again, their glances inviting, their arms beckoning. The stage quickly filled with eager men, accepting. Dartha's sultry voice added to her bodily enticements. "Come," she called richly. "The serpent has given me this fruit, and it is sweet to the taste. Come! Eat!"

Eve cringed. Her words to Adam—but in such a different context! Shame warmed her, as though her own succumbing to temptation had been sexual, rather than childishly willful. How innocent they had been, she and Adam. How innocent, in sexual ways, they had remained, long past their expulsion. How innocent, it seemed, they still were . . .

Her eyes ached with tears. She groaned inwardly with a longing that these others might know, might understand.

Many of the men who'd filled the square were responding, and others turned away to seek other excitements. Adam and she could now move forward to Ranuel.

But—and Eve's heart lurched—Ranuel, too, was scrambling for the stage.

"No!" she cried, and Adam lunged forward.

Ranuel was on the stage before they could reach him, but the huge man who'd introduced the "myth" barred his way from the door through which most of the men and all of the dancers but Dartha had already disappeared.

"But I *have* no coins!" protested Ranuel, trying feverishly to push past.

"The fruit of Dartha," the big man said, not without humor, "is not without price!"

"Ranuel!" Adam called. "My son! *No!*"

He had heard. Eve knew by his sudden stiffening. But he wouldn't turn. A long-forgotten image of small, stubborn Cain jabbed at her memory.

Ranuel would certainly have gone, but for the stolid man. Eve silently thanked God that he had no money.

But Dartha was moving forward sinuously. Her voice warm with laughter, and perhaps with longing for something long lost, she said, "This one, Ratim—this one I take without payment. I will teach him tenderly . . . how fruit should taste."

Ratim shrugged, turning his attention to Adam, struggling to the stage. "Unless you have coins, old man," he said carelessly, "you squander your energy."

Seeming to collapse within himself, Adam called pleadingly, "Son—son—don't spill your seed into such a vile vessel!"

Ranuel never turned. The curtain swished behind him. From within came the sounds of women's laughter, teasing and excited.

Poor Tarelle, thought Eve.

On the silent walk back to the donkey and cart, her soul was weighted with a thousand sad images of hopes dashed, of love betrayed, of innocence sullied, of sin's promises embraced—only to have those promises turned to ashes of regret.

For Ranuel, it seemed, the ashes would be delayed.

"I regret that I'm hurting Tarelle," he said, when he returned the next midmorning. "But I could never marry her now." His eyes glowed. "Love and desire for Dartha are like flame licking through my veins. I must have her, again and again."

"And when she casts you aside for someone else who's young and stupid?"

Ranuel's head lifted stubbornly. "I'm going, my father. Nothing you can say will stop me. You could lock me behind bars, or shut me in a well, or tie me, or—"

But Adam was shaking his head in defeat, and Eve's heart yearned toward him.

Ranuel's expression lightened. "Whenever I can," he promised. "Whenever we happen to be near—"

Adam turned and strode away.

Eve wanted to, but couldn't. She accepted her son's quick hug, returned his kiss, and watched him ride away, still confident with the promises of Dartha's love. To him, it must look shining. Only their greater experience with disillusionment allowed them to see it for the tarnished, worthless thing it was.

This birth was more difficult, even, than Meshanath's had been. The pain more searing. The sense of reality and well-being more elusive. In those fragments of time when she was aware of Ayra and could focus on her expression, Eve saw worry that verged on terror.

But I will live, Eve told herself stubbornly. *I will bear yet another son for Adam, in his image.*

This would be a son to replace Ranuel, gone already four months.

She tried to say that, to reassure Ayra, but the syllables were sluggish, disjointed. Unintelligible. Finally, she gave up the effort and concentrated on the pain.

Such pain!

She heard a scream of agony—twisting, reverberating, shredding.

It was hers.

She heard someone calling out to God for some end to the pain.

It was she.

She heard someone calling for Kara—who was Kara?

There were hands on her—comforting, testing, assisting.

Kara's hands?

Enmeshed in the puzzle, she determined to withdraw from the pain, not to breathe, not to struggle, not to push, not to worry about the baby. Let those hands take care of the baby.

"*Motherrrrr!*"

The word twisted and contorted, just as her screams had found new shapes of terror—but *she* couldn't have called that word, since she had no mother. *She* was the mother of all living. Adam had pronounced that title.

It *was* Adam who had done it, wasn't it? Not God? Or Kara?

Who was Kara?

The voice intruded again, shattering her peace, her withdrawal. "*Mother! Push! Push! Pushhhhhhhh!*"

Why didn't those hands, that voice, this babe all just go away and leave her alone? She needed peace. She needed time for contemplation in some spot quiet and beautiful . . . like Eden. Yes, she needed Eden! Eden without the serpent.

"MOTHER! MOTHER! MOTHER! PUSH-PUSH-PUSH-PUSH-PUSH—"

Like the words, the hands had multiplied. There were thousands of them, like the thousands of people who had come from Adam's seed through her, through their children, and who populated the world. She didn't know, or care to know, most of them. She didn't know these thousand hands, either. She pushed at them, wanting to be insistent. But she hadn't the strength for insistence. Petulance would have to do.

"Alone," she gasped. "Leave . . . alone . . ."

There was a long, loud, distorted sigh of sound. "She lives!"

"Kara?" she asked. Was it Kara who lived?

"Who's Kara?" someone asked, and the syllables took those tangled turns, once more.

They didn't know, either, who Kara was. She made a muttering sound of frustration and sought the peace again, but something was hurting her. Something was tearing within her, setting her entrails on fire. Something horrible and vicious and—

The scream again.

Hers.

The hands again.

Whose?

The pain, the pain, the pain, the pain, the pain—

And then a cry different from the other cries. Angrier. Louder. Closer, it seemed, and less twisted.

Is that Kara? she wondered, and raised her head to see.

The descent into blackness was unplanned, swift, and total.

In the days that followed, she knew moments of wakefulness. Hands washed and fed her. Hands comforted her. Voices spoke softly in words she didn't try to interpret.

As her periods of wakefulness lengthened, something small and wiggling was sometimes laid near her. Once, she opened one eye to look. It was a babe. An ugly one. Red and fat-cheeked, with a mouth that mewed unpleasantly. She wondered idly whose babe it was.

More often, though, she wondered about Kara.

A face still eluded her. Specific memories avoided her. The energy to ask Adam failed her. Besides, she was never sure when the hands and the voice were his and not Ayra's, or those of some stranger.

Sometimes she thought of sad things, and cried weakly. She thought most often of Tarelle, when she'd learned of Ranuel's desertion. She thought of Tarelle's face breaking into strange planes, her body sagging. She remembered catching her.

Now, she couldn't catch anyone. Anything. She couldn't even catch the elusive answer to the question most troubling her.

Who was Kara?

Tarelle had tried to kill herself.

She'd run to the cliffs. And though Eve and Adam had both pleaded with her, though she'd stood for long frantic moments in terrible indecision, she had, at last, flung herself from the edge, shrieking.

The scream had sounded like Ranuel's name, like a sob, like all the pains and sadnesses Eve had known in all her life. All accumulated, kneaded together. It had sounded like betrayal. Like blackness and desolation. Like the moments when she and Adam had fled that path from Eden. Like life without love. Without praise of God.

In the beginning, God created . . .

Had God created Kara?

Of course God had created Kara! God had created everything! And He had seen that it was good. Good.

"Good."

The word had leapt from her thoughts and taken shape in a voice. *Whose* voice?

"She's better today."

Who was better today?

"Kara?" she asked. And, miraculously, her word had sound and shape, too. "*Kara?*" she asked more loudly, testing her power.

"Do I *sound* like a sheep?" asked Adam, laughter tender in his voice.

She relaxed, smiling. Of course! That was who Kara had been! A sheep she had loved, hundreds and hundreds of years ago . . .

She slept.

For the first time in weeks, it was a natural sleep.

Tarelle had not died.

After frantic, agonized scrambling down the treacherous rocks, through the vicious brambles, they had found her crumpled and bleeding at the foot of the cliffs. As broken in body as she had been in spirit.

Seth had taken her into his home. Healing that fractured body seemed a likelier prospect than healing her wounded emotions.

The light, he said, was gone from her eyes. When she spoke, there was only heaviness in her voice. She lay limp and unresponsive, except to reiterate her wish for death. There was no reason for life without Ranuel, she had said. And as for God—if He truly existed, and if He truly cared—where had He been when Ranuel was tempted?

Eve sat on a cushioned seat Ayra had prepared for her in the early spring shadow, a heavy shawl about her shoulders for warmth. She watched as the baby, a girl, Anetha, still rather red and ugly, lay blinking at sunlight and waving her uncoordinated arms. Eve wondered if this child would grow to be godly, like Tarelle, and be injured by life, or if she would early learn that temptation embraced leads to an easier path than does temptation resisted.

"Only in the immediate sense," God's voice chided gently, "does yielding bring ease."

He was right, of course.

And yet she had watched the sinful daughters of the city as they flaunted themselves—hips swaying loosely; lips slightly open, full and wet; eyes encased in heavy cosmetics, brazen and sultry. They had seemed easy, untortured, even content.

"Not content," God intruded. "Separated from me, they can know only turmoil."

She had never before thought to assess what pain lay hidden beneath their artful exteriors. Only when she saw someone frightened, like the child at the carnival, had she felt a caring. A protectiveness.

Perhaps even Dartha—

Her lip curled at thought of the whore, tugging Ranuel toward sin.

But she forced herself past her revulsion.

Perhaps even Dartha knew the burning of shame and guilt, the darkness of lost hope.

Like a moment caught from time and set apart, she remembered Dartha's attitude—almost of longing, as she promised to teach Ranuel tenderly. Perhaps her own training had lacked all tenderness. Perhaps she felt herself forever the victim—

Harshly, Eve discarded any shred of sympathy for the woman. Ranuel was the real victim.

No.

Tarelle was the real victim.

"They have all turned from me," God sighed, "but not forever."

Eve was weary. Her thoughts had gone full circle, with nothing changed. Ranuel was gone, perhaps forever. Surely he must be disillusioned by now. Surely, incapable of coming home, admitting error. And Tarelle would limp forever as a result of her injuries. Even worse was the crippling of her spirit.

Nothing changed, Eve thought.

"Dear Eve. Be patient."

Patience. Patience! Was that all God could offer her?

"Ayra!" she called weakly.

Nothing changed, and she so weary that she ached and throbbed and yearned for the oblivion of sleep.

"*Ayra!*" she called, more plaintively.

"I'm here, Mother." The aging hands supported her, moving her slowly toward her bed. Her mind sagged. Tiredness and dimness and hopelessness roared within her.

Nothing changed. All that tiring concern. And nothing changed.

And yet, just as she drifted toward sleep, through the dimness shone a plan she'd mention to Seth when he visited again.

If Tarelle could come here, if she could know that she was needed . . . if, perhaps, Anetha's care could become her responsibility, perhaps that limping of her spirit would find some healing.

Stubbornly, Eve didn't thank God for the plan. She was too drained to listen to any more urging toward patience.

It was summer once again. Anetha was six months old, and grown a little prettier. More rosy, now, than red. Her smile more shaped. Her cooing soft and given eagerly in response to any attention she could garner. Her hands more controlled, her movements purposeful. Her eyes alert, intelligent.

She'll do, Eve thought, and regretted the time she'd lost through the babe's early weeks—time spent in her own healing. Not that the child had suffered by it. Ayra, she knew, had filled the gap. And now Tarelle.

Tarelle.

Eve watched her gently. She moved with grace made more appealing by the slight hesitation, the almost imperceptible hitch in her stride. The shattered arm had healed well. Eve had to look closely to note where the bone bulged oddly. It was only when reaching far above her head, as when carrying a pot of water, that she must use—always—the uninjured arm. And, fortunately, the scars and bruises on her face had faded long ago, leaving her as lovely as before. Lovelier, perhaps, since pain had brought maturity to her features.

But what of the scars and bruises in her heart, Eve wondered. Were they healed, as well? Or was the healing, which suggested itself in smiles and glowing eyes as she played with Anetha, merely superficial?

How she loved the child! And how Anetha returned that love in near-worship. When life displeased her, she sought the comfort of Tarelle's arms. When a bee stung her, it was Tarelle who carefully removed the stinger, who smoothed the salve across the wound. When she skinned her knees while crawling, it was Tarelle who treated the abrasion, first by washing, then by kissing, then with the healing salve.

Eve felt no jealousy. Only relief. She was weak, still, and very, very tired. Too tired to minister unflaggingly to the needs of a child. She was grateful, indeed, that Anetha needed her so seldom, and that Tarelle showed such love. She was happy for Tarelle, too—that the love she should soon have been feeling for and from a child of her own had found a willing target.

But it was unhealthy, she worried sometimes, that Tarelle thought *only* of Anetha—never of a love that might uproot and supplant whatever of Ranuel remained in her heart. Adam had shown Eve, often, how an unharvested crop rotted in the ground. Untended, what could have been rich harvest, nourishment, the seeds of future harvest, could lie in black slime, scarcely resembling once-living vegetation.

Could Tarelle's discarded love for Ranuel be festering within her—an ugly, hidden thing?

Eve frowned. It wasn't for lack of suitors that Tarelle remained still unwed. Apparently, Ranuel's rejection and the tragedy of her near-death had attracted, rather than frightened away, other potential loves. But when such a suitor presented himself, while she wasn't impolite, she managed to communicate disinterest in gentler ways.

Seth was concerned, Eve knew, about this blighted granddaughter. He watched her with worried eyes, and drew her often into prayer, which she endured politely. When Ranuel's name was mentioned, an unaccustomed hardness settled in Seth's eyes. Still, when Eve pleaded with him, he prayed for Ranuel, too. That he might continue to seek God in a godless land. That God might work in his heart, proving his need for repentance.

Never, though, did Seth pray for Ranuel's return.

Nor did Adam.

And Eve, when she thought of it, weighed the probable results. And, finding Tarelle a closer, dearer concern to her than was this wayward son, she prayed only for his safety and his eventual happiness.

Another harvest time.

The tender, bristling blossoms crowning the thistles with beauty had dimmed, had lost their purpleness to brown, had spread and furred and opened silvered strands, becoming fluffy seeds that enchanted Anetha with their gentle touch and erratic flights.

Over a year since Ranuel had gone.

Tarelle was blooming. Less often did she break off her singing to fall into thoughtfulness and silent withdrawal. Less often did she sit in shadows and stroke her stiff arm contemplatively.

Eve wondered what had promoted the greater healing. Time, Anetha, or Ben?

Ben was a gentle man, older than Tarelle by sixty years or more, widowed when his three grown daughters were still small. He yearned for sons, still. And while he admitted that the memory of his wife remained a pain beneath his rib cage, he was sure he could carry love for another woman.

He and Tarelle had met as he led his youngest grandson in his first faltering steps beside a stream to watch fish. Tarelle was there with Anetha, who'd rather try to catch than watch the swift glints of silver and gold that cut the water. Eve was with them, resting, as she always seemed to do these days.

Laughing, Tarelle had just saved Anetha from a watery grave for the third time. The child was dripping, chortling, still struggling to make the fourth try. Smiling, Eve adjusted her weight to ease a muscle, and became aware of Ben's approach.

That he had been watching them was obvious from the intentness of his scrutiny. And it was not Eve who claimed his attention, nor the adventurous child, nor the fish.

Ahhh, Eve thought comfortably, and smiled within herself. Still young, he'd be a good provider for this girl who was closer to her than many of her daughters had ever been. Handsome, he wasn't flawless, and so would fail to remind her of Ranuel. He adjusted his pace to the child's, which spoke of the patience Ranuel had always lacked.

Ahhhh.

They spoke their vows one late afternoon when harvest sheaths stood in neat rows, their gold ignited by that vivid sunlight synonymous with the season. Insects hummed incessantly in breast-high grasses, still unmown. Tarelle carried a spray of asters and ripe wheat. A crown of daisies and alfalfa rested on her luxuriant hair, which was brushed to a gleaming shine. All through the ceremony, all through the celebration that followed, her glance and Ben's clung hungrily.

It was not, Eve thought, a physical hunger, but an emotional one. Her heart swelled, and she knew an energy unfelt since Ranuel's desertion. Theirs would be a home that would know love refined by pain. There, gentleness would reign. God would be held close and precious. She breathed a wordless prayer of gratitude, knowing with certainty that smacked a bit of betrayal that Ben would cherish Tarelle as Ranuel would have been incapable of doing.

Ranuel returned just weeks later, when the final crops had been gathered, the animal pens reinforced against the coming chill.

Eve was turning drying halves of fruits, while Anetha, on her own small bench in the corner, sang a bit mournfully. As she worked, Eve had heard Adam's hammer blows, muted by distance, and the annoying buzz of a late fly.

She hadn't heard hoofbeats or footsteps, but suddenly she knew that he was there. Slowly, she freed her hands, bracing herself for what she might see, searching for what she must say.

"Mother," Ranuel said, and fell to his knees, clutching her hand to his lips.

She had expected that he might look haggard. Older.

But, except for a healed scar that angled from left eyebrow to earlobe, his perfection was unmarred. He seemed firm-fleshed, well fed.

When he raised his eyes to look into her face—ah, then the difference showed. She saw the sadness, the certain print of pain met, endured, perhaps defeated.

He stood, then, looking down at her, still holding her hand.

She hadn't remembered that he'd been so tall.

"I've come home," he said simply.

And she knew that he couldn't stay.

Anetha had noticed him, by then, and sat huddled, wide-eyed, thumb in her mouth. Ranuel smiled. "You were pregnant when I—" He broke off, clearing his throat.

Never before had he betrayed nervousness.

"Anetha," Eve said.

He raised a brow.

"Her name is Anetha."

He nodded, moving to stand by the window. Clearly, his mind was on other matters.

Tarelle, she knew, as clearly as though he'd spoken her name. And, just as clearly, she knew that she'd protect Tarelle from this further emotional assault. Ranuel, who'd shattered her before, couldn't be allowed to cloud her new joy.

He sank to a bench, but stiffly.

"Have you eaten?" she asked.

He nodded abstractedly. "There were a few apples, still."

She was glad of the excuse for meaningful movement.

He sat, watching, as she prepared bread and cheese and meat. When he ate, it was with his old appetite. And when he finished, it was with his old determination that he said, "I must see Tarelle."

She shook her head tiredly, and the ancient stubbornness settled on his features.

So he had not yet suffered enough to teach him patience.

Then he sighed, his expression relaxing, the pain once more apparent. His voice broke as he said, "How terribly I must have hurt her."

She didn't speak, just sat on another bench and waited tensely, thrashing about in her mind for words that might urge him to leave. Forever.

"It was only when someone rejected me that I could begin to understand."

The air vibrated with silence. Anetha, still tentative, remained in her corner. The hammer blows had ceased. Eve wondered dully if Adam might be coming in, and what he might say to Ranuel. What he might do.

"I love her," he said softly.

"Dartha?" she asked, keeping her voice casual, knowing that he had not meant Dartha. Almost, she felt guilt for the quick stab of pain that contorted his features.

But it was with sad softness that he said, "Not Dartha."

Again, silence stretched between them. Endless silence, it seemed to Eve. She shifted, trying to do it quietly.

"Tarelle," he said. "I love Tarelle." Another pause. "I have always, I think, loved Tarelle."

Anger stirred within her at this manner men had of calling lust love until it no longer suited their purposes. Or until they were denied.

"Where is she?" he asked abruptly. His glance never wavered from her face.

Should she lie? *Could* she lie?

His eyes narrowed, demanding an answer.

She began quietly, "When you left . . ."

That swift pain again.

"She . . ." She drew a deep breath and plunged ahead. "The cliffs—beyond the ridge—she . . ."

His eyes widened slowly, an awareness there coexisting with fresh pain.

"She threw herself from the cliff," Eve finished quickly.

Anguished, he dropped his head into his hands and sobbed.

Automatically, she stroked his shoulder, offering comfort which required no thought. He thought Tarelle was dead. He thought he'd killed her. Was it cruel or essential to encourage that belief?

If she were to tell him the truth—that Tarelle had survived the fall, but had only now survived his desertion, that she had found new happiness with someone else—would he, then, leave? Or would he demand to see her? And if he did, what of Tarelle? What of Ben?

"She was so beautiful," he was sobbing. "So gentle. So graceful. Like willow fronds when she walked. I have dreamed so often of seeing her again. Of coming upon her silently, watching her walk beside the stream—"

And Eve knew what she must do. Into her mind rose an image of Tarelle, her limp exaggerated when she was aware of others, watching.

She could tell him that Tarelle still lived, could give him that chance to wound her again, and—in the end—he would turn from her, because more than her soul beauty, he had loved the physical.

She stood briskly. "Your father has never forgiven you," she said, forcing herself to be harsh. "Nor have I. We loved Tarelle, and would have loved your children by her. But you chose a harlot above her, above us, and you wasted your seed in defiled ground. I have fed you as I would have fed a stranger, passing through. I pray only for your good . . . that God walk with you always. But I cannot—I *will* not—ask you to stay."

He had flinched with her words, and now he stood, reeling slightly. "It is a portion of my punishment," he said, and there was acceptance in his tone.

She longed to pull him to her breast and comfort him and speak a love he could never kill.

But she had more than her own instincts to consider.

Her eyes filled with tears. "Where will you go, my son?"

"There are cities, several of them, between here and the sea. There are fields for tilling, and meadows where a man may pull his thoughts together, and repair himself."

A man. Yes, she thought. Whatever else he had become, he was now a man.

She reached to touch his arm. "I must know. Do you remember God? Do you speak the Creation Hymn? Do you pray?" Her heart leapt as he nodded without hesitation.

"Each night," he said, "these months I've been wandering, building the courage to face you, to face—" Another spasm of pain caught in his eyes. "Each night, I have done both."

She nodded softly. "It is good."

Just on the point of leaving, he asked, without turning, "One more thing I must know."

She waited, tensing.

"If . . . if Tarelle still lived, would you have told me where to find her?"

She braced herself against the table. "That is something," she answered carefully, "that I cannot answer."

Nine

"It always troubles me," Adam called quaveringly from his shaded spot in the grape arbor, "how much I forget."

How tremulous his voice has grown these past years, Eve thought. Of course, hers had, too. And they were both quavering in more than voice.

"It always troubles me," he said, "how much things change."

Anetha, almost one hundred herself, smiled from her large loom, reassembled on the porch when she and her youngest children had arrived for an extended visit. She'd grown into a gentle woman who loved her family and her work and considered little beyond that sphere.

Denati, Adam and Eve's own youngest, sat near Adam's arbor, fashioning hooks for fishing. "How many are there of us now, Mother?" he asked.

She shook her head and clucked laughingly.

"Oh, I don't mean altogether! I mean"—he waved vaguely—"just my brothers and sisters and me."

That was nearly as impossible! Over the years, so many names once always on her tongue had passed from memory. There were some, she thought, straining, who very early had traveled to distant fields, establishing cities. And, more recently, so many others, following . . .

Denati said comfortably, "If you can't remember, it's all right."

"Of course I can remember!"

Placing a finished hook to one side, he seemed to wait.

She added crossly, "How could a person ever forget a thing like that?"

He shrugged. And began another hook.

"It always troubles me . . ." Adam began. And stopped.

He's drowsing again, Eve thought.

Anetha called from the porch, "Why don't you take your nap, too, Mother? When he wakes, he'll be needing you again."

Slowly, awkwardly, she pushed to her feet. "Especially a mother," she finished. "A mother couldn't possibly . . ."

As her voice faded off, she thought, *I'm doing the same thing Adam does. And it always annoys me so!* She turned back to offer a complete sentence to Denati—but he seemed content enough, humming, working with the hooks.

Maneuvering the once-easy path to the house, to the bedroom, she chuckled. *Children. Always wanting to know about the past.*

As she lowered herself to her pallet, she was vaguely aware of Anetha standing by, hands ready, in case she might be needed. "I can manage," Eve said a bit stiffly, and finished in her thoughts, *just as I always manage when you're nowhere around.*

There was an arrogance about young people. Even when they were motivated by kindness and love, even when they tried to be subtle. Their very smoothness and vitality and flexibility and color were a constant, insistent reminder of what was forever gone.

And yet their enchantment with past events never waned. And that was good. There was much about the past, she knew, that the children must learn if the future were to be better than the present. Yet, all these centuries, she and Adam had tried to pass on the important lessons, and only a few had picked them up. Seth had done well. Many of his descendants remained godly—had, in fact, formed a group that worshiped Yahweh, their name for God. Seth had explained that when they spoke simply of "God," most people asked, "Which one?" The name *Yahweh* set Him apart from all false gods.

And there were many such gods, a fact Eve found even more troubling than Adam's lapses of memory. Most were shabby little figures, formed of clay or iron, which just squatted wherever they were set and smiled their silly little smiles, getting a bit rusty-looking if offerings of flowers were left past their freshest. But some supposedly made their homes in the sky, sending winds and drought and lightning when they were displeased about something. And others lived in the earth, deciding whether wheat or thistles grew. And there were others in the streams and stones and trees, and—she supposed—in the frogs and caterpillars and crickets, as well.

However energetically Adam or Seth or Enoch or any of the others had pleaded for sanity, these foolish people couldn't seem to understand that one God had made everything: that worshiping these man-devised substitutes was worse than useless, it was also an insult to Him.

Surely the cult that troubled Eve most was the one that worshiped her.

Oh, they didn't realize they were worshiping *her*. If they'd passed her on the public road, they'd have cursed her aside as a nuisance. They'd have railed at her for her slowness, for her age. (It seemed that young people grew increasingly disrespectful.)

However, this cult worshiped the "goddess" they called "Mother of All Living" in disgusting ceremonies that featured fertility rites.

Although Seth had carefully tried to shield her from many of the details, she'd heard rumors . . .

Sex, it seemed, was the basis of the total religion. Sex without love, without rules, without limits. Sex that had become for some the only goal in life, and for others the ultimate tyranny.

And it was Eve, or their distorted image of Eve, who ruled their degradation. Many said that she *demanded* it, if she were to look favorably on the productivity of their soil and the richness of their wombs.

Because of their licentious practices, she had heard Seth telling Adam, new diseases had sprung up among them. Foul diseases, linked directly to their excesses. Diseases that could be spread through marriage to innocent, even God-fearing, partners.

There was so much sadness, thought Eve, resting on her pallet. So much rumor—of giants roaming the land, forming unnatural alliances with young women, corrupting many who had been pledged from birth to Yahweh.

So much darkness. So much evil. So much sinning. So much of hopelessness—

And yet so much of hope.

For each doubt she and Adam expressed concerning the future of humanity, there was a matching joy. Seth speaking to ever-growing crowds about Yahweh. Seth's godly line—leading to Enoch and Methusaleh. As long as such men walked the earth, God would be represented.

She slipped into sleep thinking of Enoch. He had asked to visit that afternoon, and his tones had been vibrant, full of excitement . . .

Her slumber was shallow, often disturbed by small sounds of nature, by the clacking of Anetha's shuttle, by the memory of Denati asking, "How many are there of us, Mother?" Then her studious attempt to trace the line, in order. First, of course, there'd been Cain. Cain, setting his small lip stubbornly. Cain saying, "Let me do it, Mother!" and carrying, with buckling knees, a weight far too heavy for his slight frame.

A turning, a shifting, on the lumpy pallet.

Too hot for sleeping, surely.

And so much to do.

With Enoch coming . . . there were those special cakes he loved. The savory ones. One of her own children had loved them best, as well.

Deri? No, Deri was the one who'd delighted most in giving—who, when she was scarcely tall enough to toddle, had raised clouds of dust that nearly obscured her. Quiet, she had been, and inward. Seldom saying what she liked or didn't like, but simply trying to please.

And Sael. Sael had always yearned to please—to please Cain. To polish his drum. To do his tasks—even the heavy work, when she could convince him that he should allow her to.

Poor Sael, her star extinguished before she'd ever had a chance to shine, save with reflected light. So sad. So sad.

So many gone. Most leaving eagerly, reaching for those elusive promises of the future. Some going casually, not realizing how complete and definite the break would be. Some going sadly, clinging with tears and hugs and promises—prolonging touch and agony of parting.

Like Janyi. Dear child. Taller than Eve by a hand's length, always so close, both physically and emotionally, that Eve sometimes felt smothered.

"I need a—" Eve would begin, and before she could complete the request, Janyi was off to find the needed tool, or spice, or bowl.

"How does she *do* that?" one of the other daughters had asked, with just an inflection of jealousy. "Why isn't she ever *wrong?*"

And another had teased, "Oh, she *is* wrong, but Mother just changes her needs to fit."

"When she was young," Adam growled once, after Eve had stumbled over the bulky girl twice in an hour, "it was amusing to see her act the burr to your fleece. But now . . ."

"She means well." But Eve had sighed, as she rubbed her bruised shin, and found herself anticipating that time when Janyi would cling to a husband—

though she hoped, for his sake, not with an equal tenacity.

Yet, despite everything, Eve's tears equaled Janyi's in volume once the cart was packed and ready, and Janyi's husband eager to be off.

It was so hard to let them go.

There had been Ranuel, banished by Eve's untruth—or, rather, by her calculated skirting of the truth.

Had Ranuel ever returned? Her memory churned painfully. There'd been a day—or had she imagined it? Had she so often needed his return, his happiness complete, his attitudes so changed, that she might erase from conscience that loving lie, that she'd imagined—?

She didn't know.

But an image shimmered, like a reflection in a pool, startled by some small stirring.

Ranuel, already grayed about the temples, arriving in a cart that bulged with many tousle-headed youngsters of varied sizes—all giggling, poking, jumping, singing, while their plump mother smiled.

Ranuel saying, "I knew, my mother. From the beginning, I was certain that Tarelle still lived. All the time I'd been with Dartha, I'd felt that tugging—a connection—as though she wouldn't, or couldn't, quite release me."

Pausing, he shook his head. "At first, I resented her. I wanted her to leave my mind. To let me be. Then, later, she was salvation, tugging me toward sanity. Toward life, when living seemed impossible. And then, that day I came to you, I knew that I needed to see her. To draw strength from her again. To drain her spirit for the healing of my own." Another pause. "I thank you for not telling me."

Her lie, absolved. Deception justified.

But had it really happened? Or had she so required an absolution that her mind had spun a fantasy?

Another turning.

A moment of slumber, terminated as a fly lit on her forehead, then launched new flight.

Ranuel. Did he yet live? He surely must; he'd not be old. Anetha was a child when he'd returned from Dartha. Had it been Ranuel who'd loved the savory cakes?

Or Dan, or Pharim, or Meshanath. Meshanath had delighted in anything remotely edible. Pharim—alarming that she couldn't capture Pharim's face. So long, so very long since he'd left her life. And Lese. And Kim. Saru. Um. Marik. Lunt . . . so many, gone. So many, dimly inhabiting the verges of memory gone dull.

Names fled through her thoughts in blurred succession, and—though she snatched at them—she felt them spin away. Arusha, Durel, Bern, Matil, Zun, Benij, Palie, Rynadab, Osanti, Relia, Lepi, Delia, Elena, Ruel, Kae . . .

Another memory surfaced, clear and vivid. Three children playing instruments with Seth, in cadence to the Hymn.

So lovely.

How could they think, Adam and she, that hope was gone, when such sweet purity existed, still, in many of their descendants?

Ralisha. Then surely it had been Ralisha who loved the savory cakes.

Or had it been Ayra? Surely she . . .

Who had it been who'd midwifed lovingly so many of her children?

Ahhh. *That* had been Ayra!

And Ayra, too, was dead. As so many sweet babies she had spanked to crying had grown to die. Some dead in childbirth. Some in drunkenness. Others in quarreling. Some victim to those odious diseases caused by shame.

How could they think, Adam and she, that there was any hope when rampant sin existed? Continued to corrupt?

And Ralisha: Had she died, too? Was it she who had withered, unmarried and unblessed by children, still mourning the love Cain's grandson's grandson had not been free to offer?

Surely, then, Ralisha had been the one who loved the savory cakes!

Or had it been one of those numerous others? Their names eluded her, but their faces swarmed before her in all the expressions of childhood, and their darker actions faded through memories of their love.

Once sleep completely overtook her, she overslept.

When Denati woke her, tickling her forehead with a scarlet feather, she knew by the slant of the sun that it was too late to start the savory cakes.

"I haven't slept," she told him, creaking to her feet, "but only closed my eyes while I counted, to answer your question."

"It doesn't matter, Mother." He stroked her hand.

"But a question deserves an answer."

"It was an idle question, not worthy of your answering."

"Still, I've been counting."

He waited, not expectantly, she thought, and she continued with asperity and anguish. "A mother could never forget."

"Besides," he said, "my brother's grandson's grandson Enoch has arrived and waits with Father. He says he has a surprise."

Enoch seemed to glow with a light from within. The warmth, illumination, depth, and compassion in his eyes reminded Eve vaguely of someone . . . someone long, long ago.

Of God?

She smothered the thought, apologizing wordlessly to God.

But then, perhaps, it had been Enoch God had meant—meant for what? The thought wouldn't (or couldn't) complete itself.

Still, she could think of no other *person* who had communicated constantly the wisdom, the love, the control, which never seemed to diminish in Enoch's day-by-day responses. In many people—in some of their own children, and in Adam, certainly—she'd seen Enoch's characteristics in flashes. But, in Enoch, they were sustained. Unswerving. He was, of all men, a good man.

If Enoch had been in Eden, she'd sometimes thought, he'd never have considered savoring forbidden fruit, no matter who had urged him. She at once loved him for his unflagging goodness and was mildly annoyed by it. And she was too tired, at her age, to analyze either reaction.

"Enoch," she said, warmly, "and . . . ?" She had momentarily forgotten.

"Methuselah," the young man himself supplied, moving to her and capturing her hand in his. "I come with my father with news of great importance!" In his eyes was the brilliance she'd so often glimpsed in Adam's.

Long ago, she sighed in her thoughts. Now, Adam sat vacant-eyed. Agitated. Apparently unaware that he was not alone.

"You are the father of a new son," she guessed. An age-old anguish tinged her voice. The excitement when a daughter was born was never so joyous. How long she'd hoped and prayed that generations would erase the inequality.

But Methuselah was speaking. "We have named him Lamech."

"A good name," she said. (How many times she'd spoken those same words, trying to make each saying seem the first.) "A strong name, and proud."

Enoch's laughter was warm and rich. "She said the same of your name, my son." He came to her, then, falling to his knees and bowing over her hands.

She lifted one, touching his head in a kind of blessing. "I said it of your name, too, when you were red and squalling." Creakingly, she bent to kiss him. Her back caught, and she tried to hide the pain. But no one hid pain, of any variety, from Enoch. Gently, he helped her to a seat.

"It always troubles me," Adam was saying, "when I forget . . ."

They waited.

"He has forgotten," Eve said sadly, "what it is that he forgets." She sighed, feeling tears gather in her eyes, feeling too weary to deny them. "We are so old, Enoch. Old and tired. Like faded petals, withering and drying on the stem."

"Yet still emitting fragrance," he said softly. "Surely you've noticed how the fragrance often multiplies when blooms are well matured?"

She chuckled drily. Well matured. Is that what they were, she and Adam? Not old. Not ancient. Not decrepit.

Well matured.

"It always troubles me—" Adam's voice broke off as Anetha entered with a tray of mugs, their patterns blurred by the frost of escaping coldness.

Walking with studied care, his tongue between his teeth, Denati followed with a second tray. Savory cakes, Eve noted, and stiffened, renewing the pain in her back.

"I remembered, my mother," Anetha said, apologetically, "that when Enoch visits—"

"It is good, my daughter," Eve said formally. Ice lay in her tones, and as she tallied Anetha's pain at having failed to please, she knew herself incapable, just then, of easing it.

Later, perhaps, when her own pain at being old nad passed.

But Enoch was saying, "I have always felt that the greatest expression of love is imitation. A son imitates his father's stride, no matter the cost in comfort. A daughter imitates those skills she most admires in her mother. And as the imitation approaches the original—*ah!* These are delicious, Aunt Anetha! A tribute of the highest form to you, my grandfather's grandfather's grandmother!" He lifted the half-eaten cake in a salute that included them both.

Anetha was smiling and at ease, once more. And, Eve had to admit, the ice in her own heart was melting. How was it that, unerringly, Enoch always said the proper thing for healing wounds? If he could store that quality in casks and sell it on market days—

"I have forgotten—" Adam was peering at Enoch.

"I have come," Enoch said, "to show you something exciting!" He set aside his mug, and strode to the far corner of the porch, to a bulky packet, obviously heavy, and wrapped in a woven cloth. Methuselah tensed.

Catching some of the expectation almost palpable in the afternoon air, Eve leaned forward until the pain caught her again. Denati, she noticed, fairly panted with excitement, his hands moving as though he would tear the wrappings more quickly from the package. And Anetha, slowly and carefully, had placed the tray on a stone ledge and had stepped closer.

Only Adam seemed impervious to the air of breathlessness.

And, once the package was fully unwrapped, Eve could consider him most wise.

What were they? She tried to make sense of the uneven rectangles of hardened clay, with designs scrawled across them. At any market could be found hundreds of pots and trays designed more beautifully, by far. She leaned back, disappointed, yet feeling—as she had always felt when one of the children brought a pretty pebble or leaf or bit of elementary weaving for her admiration—that she must say something in approval.

She cleared her throat.

Adam cleared his, too, before venturing tentatively, "A little too heavy for trays, wouldn't you think, my dear Eve?"

Enoch saved her from any response, and from any counterfeit praise she might have framed. "But they aren't trays," he said. In his excitement, he omitted Adam's title—so bulky, anyway, Eve had always thought. "They're"—his voice softened richly—"they're *writing!*"

"*Writing?*"

Eve wasn't sure who had repeated the strange word; perhaps she had. What was writing? And, perhaps more important, what did it really matter?

Anetha quietly retrieved her tray and moved toward the house. Denati, lacking excuse and maturity to follow, looked after her—almost longingly, Eve thought.

"Writing!" Enoch's excitement throbbed in his voice. "Do you see this—here?" His forefinger indicated a lengthy scrawl, tangled with embellishments. He looked at each of them, waiting for affirmation.

"It's there, again," Denati noted. "And there, and there!"

"Ahhhh," purred Enoch, ruffling the boy's hair fondly. "Good lad!"

"But . . ."

It was all the encouragement Enoch had needed. "It's a word," he explained carefully. His hand moved tenderly across the tablet. "All of these are words."

But words were to be spoken. To be heard. Still, Eve tuned her attention to Enoch's words—both those she heard, and those he said were carved in clay.

"This word—the one I showed you—is *ungodly*. And that"—he pointed again—"that word is *judgment*. And that one, *Lord*. Not God. Not Yahweh. Another Lord Yahweh will one day send to, as it says here, to"—running his forefinger beneath the scrawls as he continued, it seemed he recited a litany—"to execute judgment upon all, and to convince all that are *ungodly* among them of all their *ungodly* deeds."

He paused, although additional lines still waited to be read. "Denati," he said, leaning forward eagerly, "when you have learned to understand this writing—when others have also learned—it will be possible for you to write your thoughts on such a tablet, and for others, however far away in time or place, to read and understand what it is that you have written!"

Denati sat stiffly, his mouth slightly open, and Eve saw on his face a variety of warring expressions. Disbelief. Amazement. Eagerness.

In her own mind, dulled though it sometimes was with aging, she felt a stirring of excitement. "Then this—" she ventured. "*Adam! This* could be a way to keep the Creation Hymn always before our children's children's children!"

"Exactly!" said Enoch, almost in a shout.

Adam started, grunting, and seemed with some difficulty to focus his attention on them.

Methuselah explained, "It is why we have come. To write the Creation Hymn, without the slightest error, so that it remains unchanged for all generations."

"There are times," quavered Adam, "when some lines slip away from me."

"No longer, my father," Denati said firmly. "If a line should escape memory, it can be renewed with this . . . this writing! Teach me," he said without pause, turning to Enoch. His body was braced in a position of pleading. "Teach me this writing! And tell me: From where did these words come?" He touched the tablet almost worshipfully.

Enoch said simply, "God gave them to me one day as we walked and talked together."

Eve looked up quickly to catch Enoch's compassionate glance. He shook his head almost apologetically. He knew too keenly, she thought, her own frantic efforts, and Adam's, to reestablish that tangible closeness with God. She'd felt blest and humble that a sensation of His presence had often enveloped her, and that, increasingly, she had heard His voice. Yet she had yearned for the easy physical nearness once accepted so casually. She should feel gratified that the closeness had finally returned to one who carried their blood within his veins.

But any gratitude she might feel later was overwhelmed for the moment by an anguish that verged on jealousy.

Another harvest.

Was it her imagination, or did they come more swiftly, now? One season merged with blurring speed into another, and—each few months, it seemed—another harvest.

And was it her imagination, or did Adam seem younger? The quavering was gone from his voice. And his movements, while still slow and careful, seemed more certain. When he spoke of forgetfulness now, it was to say, "Some of the lines of the litany would, at times, escape my mind. And it troubled me deeply. But Enoch has written them down!"

"I know," she would say, patting his hand. No matter that neither she nor Adam had learned to read the writing. It was for others the Hymn had been copied. She would add, "Now it shall never be forgotten."

"Enoch has removed a great burden from my mind."

"It is good," she would say—and know that it had been. That both of them could rest more easily, now that the words that had failed to find permanence in so many minds had found it in tablets of clay. No longer, at night, need either of them lie awake, repeating the phrases, searching for a word or a line that had fallen into darkness . . . and then, retrieving that, find that another had slipped from reach.

"It is good," he would repeat.

He said it many times, that day of the sacrifice, as they made preparations. Anetha worked busily at the kneading board, shaping small loaves of bread and the savory cakes Eve had asked her, especially, to bake. She sang softly—sweetly, Eve thought. Closing her eyes, she could recall a thousand such songs sung by working daughters, happy with flour and leavening, and a thousand or more songs which had sprung from her own contentment.

Denati had chosen his own lamb for sacrifice, and was washing it over and over again. *The poor lamb will be glad for the release of death,* Eve thought, half smiling.

"Tonight," Adam was saying, nearby, "tonight, Enoch will *read* the Creation Hymn!"

If they had had the written tablets to send to Cain, Eve mused, might he have run his fingers over those carved words, allowing them to sink into his heart? Could his whole line, then, have been reclaimed for the one true God?

And yet so many of those close by, where exposure to Yahweh was a constant possibility, had rejected Him.

Perhaps the tablets would have made no difference. Would make no difference now.

Or, perhaps generations from now some man or woman who had never heard the name of God would find the tablets and—

—and, she finished, her spirits sinking, would think them worthless, never having learned the meanings of such markings.

Too weary to continue that path of thought, she moved—slowly and painfully—to help Anetha with preparations for the meal.

It was quiet.

After the celebration—the music, the dancing, the greetings of those unseen since last harvest or longer; the hugs and kisses and excited sharing of events; the hoisting of children for appraisal and approval, the predictable "How he's grown! How pretty she's become!"; after the vibrant solemnity of the sacrifice; after the drama of the reading; after the prayers and spilled blood and close-watched smoke, ascending—it was quiet.

"Come walk with me," Adam suggested. His hand, as he caught hers, seemed firmer than it had been for many, many years. His closeness was as comforting as it had always been. Shored by the strength remembered, she felt her own stride firm, her own years lift.

"I have always loved you," she said.

His voice smiled. "And I have always known."

She pressed more closely to him, and their walking slowed.

It was a sweet evening. Fragrance of harvest clung to the air, and they carried with them vestiges of sacrificial smoke. In their minds, tendrils of voices twined—at least, Eve thought, in hers. She must stop this habit of attributing her thoughts to him. But so often, it seemed, they thought in concert—increasingly, as the years accumulated.

They had known so much that was shared. Shared Eden. Shared pain. Shared love. Shared fears. Shared guilts.

Strange—now that she knew so much so clearly, the reasons for shame were blurred.

They had shared so many, many children. One day, when she was feeling clearer in her memory, she'd have to remember all of them—perhaps asking Enoch to list them—and count, answering Denati's question.

It *was* Denati who had asked, wasn't it? Not Seth or Meshanath or one of the many, many others?

Might it have been Ranuel?

No. Not Ranuel. He was the one who—

"I have always meant to tell you—" Adam's voice trailed off.

"—how it pains me, still, to remember . . ."

"Remember what?" she asked, almost absently.

"That night. That night I . . . forced you." The last words were soft and pain-wracked.

She shook her head. What fancy, now, shaped his wrinkled thoughts? *"Adam—"*

"No!" He said it with the old firmness he'd sometimes exercise when both of them understood, because of God's guidelines, that she *must* listen. "Don't prattle," he said, more gently. "It was in the granary, and I'd been drinking."

You never drink, she argued, but only in her thoughts. As far, far back as her memory could reach, he'd shunned the wine so many of the others offered, on any pretext.

"It was after Cain's . . . it was after Abel's . . ."

Cain. Abel. Her memory stirred, but no firm images formed.

"Even though you forgave me. Even though God did—"

There was in his voice such anguish, such intensity, such *need,* that she wouldn't—couldn't—argue.

Forcing her voice to sound as though she understood, she comforted, "And we did. We do." She turned to him, and he closed his arms around her.

Less steadily, he said, "I didn't deserve . . ."

"I have always loved you," she said, again.

There was such a rightness there, in his arms. He must have felt it, too, for he smiled and nodded. "I thank God, continually, that He has given you to me, to be with me."

It was more than something he was saying to her, she knew. It was a litany. "And I, too, raise continual praises for His great blessings," she contributed.

"He has blessed us with the richness of many children . . ."

". . . and with their children's children . . ."

". . . seeing our blood renewed in countless generations."

Not quite countless yet, she thought, and would have smiled, but for a sudden catch in her chest—

He was waiting.

She added hurriedly, a little breathlessly, "He has enriched the earth for our sakes . . ."

". . . and from it we have wre⟨ ' food for nourishment . . ."

". . . and flax for spinning . . .'

"And from the richness of the earth have sprung our flocks and herds—"

It was her turn, she knew. And she felt the praise churning for expression.

But there was in her chest a growing *something,* more pain than ecstasy, a bursting, a thrusting . . . a tearing, a searing . . . an explosion of all former agonies commingled. Of childbirth pain—displaced; a travailing in the center of her breast. *Oh, God! Oh, Adam!*

She drew a jagged breath, then exhaled deeply, and felt herself collapsing . . . felt Adam's arms—stronger about her than they should have been— felt herself being lowered, lowered, lowered—how far could it be to the ground? . . . And the pain, the pain, the pain, the pain . . .

"Oh, God! Eve—don't *leave* me!" Adam's voice was ragged. Tortured.

She couldn't comfort him this time. The pain took everything . . . and demanded more. And how could she *not* leave when the pain pushed and pressured? The pain absorbed. Swelled and crowded and wrenched and—

"*A-dam*—"

Not *her* voice—that gasping, that croaking, that rattling—

"I know," he said, and his words were strangled with tears. "I know, my dear, sweet Eve, that you have always loved me—as I love you . . ." His arms convulsed about her, and she heard his wretched sobbing—a sobbing to embrace accumulated griefs of centuries.

Such sadness!

The sadness faded. Mellowing. Merging with echoes of music.

Such music!

It is good . . . it is good . . . it is good . . . it is good . . . The words spun through her mind, embroidering a million images of love shared, of problems solved, of laughter mingled, of beauty enjoyed. And suddenly, *yes!* She could answer Denati's question, and all of the questions anyone might ask her . . . except what Adam had mentioned . . . his having forced her. He never—

"Adam!" No longer anguished, but softer than an embrace . . .

Once before, she had known that swirling, that amplified heartbeat—but never like this. Never so like a shout, reverberating from cliff to cliff and growing . . .

"*A-dammmmmmmmmmmm!*"

"I am here."

"I am here."

Two voices, overlapping.

One Adam's, always loved.

The other, heard eternities before, and through the centuries between. But never more vibrantly. Never so welcoming.

It seemed fitting, as she slipped from Adam's tightening grip, as she lost the vision of his face . . . it was fitting, in the end as in the beginning, at the last as at the first, that she saw Him.

She arched her shoulders, stretched her arms upward in an exuberance of wakening from long, satisfying sleep. An eagerness, a joy, a delight, an aliveness brought surprised laughter bubbling to her lips.

Reaching, He drew her to her feet. Effortlessly. "I have missed you," He said.

She frowned slightly. "But You never left us!"

His words echoed gently, "I never left you."

He led her through mists touched with flower scent and muted color. And the music. A soft music, which infused her mind with phrases of love and joy and praise and thankfulness.

Looking into His face, His eyes, she felt no need to speak the words. He had heard.

She said only, "I have always loved You." And she remembered, fleetingly, that moments before, she had spoken those identical words to Adam.

Dear Adam.

Wondering when he would join them, she experienced no sense of loss, no sense of longing. Later, Adam would be there. It was enough.

"Come." God tugged at her hand.

"Oh!" The syllable burst from her lips with excitement forged by centuries of yearning. "Are we returning to—" But the name eluded her, that name which had been the fulcrum of every discontent.

"Eden," He supplied.

She nodded from politeness. The word meant nothing.

"To a place better than Eden," He promised.

Wherever He led her, she knew, would be beautiful. Perfect. Complete. His presence would make it so.

She sighed, content. Adam would come. Already, many of their children moved toward her, smiling, their shapes emerging from mist.

Her steps quickened.

God's laughter was warm. Contagious.

Mist evaporated in wisps, in tendrils, in layers.

She embraced her children.

"It is good," God said.

And Eve knew that it *was* good.